SOMEONE TO CALL BAE 3

SIREN

Cole Hart
SIGNATURE NOVELS

Someone To Call Bae 3

Mailing List

To stay up to date on new releases, plus get information on contests, sneak peeks, and more,

Go To The Website Below...

www.colehartsignature.com

❧ I ❧

DEJAH

"It's a girl."

"The fuck?" Shawnie got angry. "You ain't seeing that big ass dick my son got?"

"Sir, that's the umbilical cord," the ultrasound tech responded. "Your son is a daughter."

"Ain't this about a bitch."

"Seriously?" I looked at Shawnie with disgust. He was so fucking ghetto.

"I didn't want no girls. They too much trouble."

"Well, that's your karma for all the women you did dirty." I rolled my eyes.

The tech just looked at us like we were toxic.

"You wilding. You know I'ma love my baby regardless."

"You better."

"Umm, I will give you all a minute. Please speak with the front desk about scheduling another appointment." The tech looked at us before leaving.

"Are you really upset about us having a girl?"

"Hell fucking yeah. I've been surrounded by girls all my life. They be too emotional. The way I used to knock down bitches? I don't want no nigga fucking my daughter."

"Well, what do you want me to do? Send it back??"

"Nah, man." Shawnie rubbed my belly. "I'm feeling a type of way. But I'm happy for us."

"Let's just go." I was upset and ready to go home.

"So what, I'm not allowed to say how I feel?"

"If you want to start an argument, Shawnie, just say that."

"Whatever man."

"So what's the problem?"

"You going to the house?" Shawnie's eyes turned cold.

All day, Shawnie had been acting distant and off. I knew Shawnie wanted a son, but the way he was reacting to having a daughter was all uncalled for. I just didn't want to argue with him, I just wanted to go home.

"Whatever."

As soon as I got into the door, I went to our bedroom and laid down. My mind was swimming in my thoughts of why Shawnie was acting like this.

"I'll be back later tonight." Shawnie stood in the door of our bedroom.

"What's later?" I sat up.

"Later."

"Who is she? Keisha?"

"Why you always accusing me of cheating? And I'm tired of hearing about Keisha. If you that insecure, why you marry me?"

"Because I love you. Because I thought you loved me too."

"I do. I just got a lot going on."

"Like?"

"It's nothing. I got it handled."

"So where are you going?"

"To Keisha's..."

"Well, at least you being honest about cheating on your pregnant wife. Thank you."

"I'm not cheating. I'm picking up my niece."

"Okay. I will be in the car." I stood.

"I don't think that's a good idea." Shawnie grabbed me by the arm. "I'm not trying to have no drama. I'ma have my mom get her. I'm feeling boxed in, Dejah."

"Wow."

"It's not you. It's family shit. Shit I don't want you involved in. The less you know the better. So, if the police come asking questions, you can't tell them nothing. I'll be back." Shawnie kissed my cheek, not giving me time to react.

☙❧

I woke to hear Shawnie on the phone, but when he saw that I was up he told Ice he would hit him back.

"I did some thinking. And with everything that we been through, it's not fair for me to keep secrets from you. I'm not selling drugs no more. I will never do that shit again. I'm just helping Ice run money through a couple laundromats."

At this point, I'd rather Shawnie had said he was cheating. At least he wouldn't be risking his freedom. I wasn't even angry but disappointed. I did the last few months with Shawnie when he was in prison. I couldn't handle it then and now being his wife and the mother of his child, I knew I couldn't do it.

"So you going to risk your freedom? What about us?"

"Ice is my bro. This shit is temporary, and I know if I was in his situation I know he would have my back."

"And what if you get caught? I don't want to bring our daughter to see her dad in jail."

"I know."

"We are fine financially. We are not hurting for—"

"I said I know!" Shawnie snapped. "I'ma tell him I'm out." Shawnie didn't look my way.

"I just want us to be—" My sentence was cut short as a pain shot through my back. "Aww!" I yelped.

"Baby, you bleeding!" Shawnie pointed out as I looked and saw the crimson liquid seeping through my shorts.

I was only five months pregnant, meaning I was too far along for a miscarriage but just in the range for a stillborn. "The baby. I can't lose her."

"We ain't going to." Shawnie reached for me to help me off the bed. Shawnie was trying to keep the mood calm, but I could see the fear in his eyes as he sped to Jackson Memorial.

"Baby, I'm sorry for how I been acting. I'm sorry for being upset about our daughter," Shawnie said.

"It's okay." I gritted down on my teeth as the pain hit me again. It seemed like every five minutes the pain came back. I was praying like crazy for God to save my baby. All I wanted was to hold my daughter, but not like this.

The car was barely in park as Shawnie picked me up and ran me into the emergency room. I was in so much pain I didn't even care if anybody saw my bloody shorts. We didn't have to wait for a nurse. It only took a matter of seconds before I was being placed on gurney.

The pain was getting stronger and I found myself getting sleepy. "Sir, you can't come back here!" I heard someone yell at Shawnie.

"Nigga, you got me fucked up! That's my wife."

The nurses and doctors began to work fast as an oxygen mask went over my face and they began to hook me up to an IV and some monitors.

I guess nobody wanted to go toe to toe with Shawnie, so the medical staff allowed him to hold my hand as they ran me down to the hall. The urge to take a nap was getting stronger as I was rushed into a surgical room. Shawnie refused to leave me and security had to be called to remove him. I was warm and numb and had no desire to react.

"She's coding!" were the last words Shawnie heard before being escorted away. They were the last words I heard too as my eyes got heavy and I succumbed to sleepiness that took over my being.

2

KEISHA

"If only your mama could see you right now." I smiled at Sidney as I admired the pristine white Milla Nova wedding dress she was wearing. The white-gold tiara with purple sapphires and green emeralds accented the soft ringlets pinned to the right side of Sidney's head. Sidney took a deep breath as Bernard placed the French silk veil over her face. She looked so lovely as radiance emitted from her aura as Bernard took Sidney's arm into his to head to the courtyard for the ceremony.

I was happy to be a part of this amazing day, and I was honored that Sidney wanted me to be here. Even if her ass was only a few years younger than me. Sidney's mother died when she was younger, and I was more than happy to stand in her mother's place. I finally was at a place in my life where I was happy, and Bernard and Sidney had become my family.

Sidney was trying to remain calm, but here she was about to marry the man she had known for the majority of her life. Just the thought of it had me thinking of Shawnie. This could have been us. But he moved on and so had I.

I watched Sidney try to get her emotions in control, but Jhene Aiko was singing her heart out in the song "While We're

Young," and when she finally laid eyes on her fiancé, she was a crying mess.

I imagined myself walking down the aisle one day. I tried to imagine it being Bernard, but my mind wouldn't let me, as I couldn't stop picturing Shawnie. Standing at the altar stood the man that had shaped me into the strong woman that I had become. The father of my future beautiful, chocolate-hued babies. The man that I fought abuse, rape, and depression to see again. The man that would go to war with the devil behind me. The man who was willing to walk away from a multi-million-dollar drug industry for me. The man that possessed my heart. And more importantly, the man that simply made me feel like the world could be safe again. My imaginary wedding ended as I focused back on the wedding.

You know I'm down to ride
I'm giving you my heart, please don't break it
Take it and lock it up and put me in your pocket, love
Alright, right by your side
I'll go everywhere you go
You know I'll go, I'll go
Everywhere you go
Baby while we're young

The courtyard of the Jaya House Mansion was absolutely beautiful. Money was not an option as Bernard dropped over one hundred thousand dollars on the wedding, honeymoon, and flying out his family from Texas for the five-day festivities that led up to the wedding. The courtyard was vibrant with lush purple and lime green orchids and other tropical flowers flown in from the Bahamas.

As a matter of fact, the entire wedding was tropical themed. The Jaya House had a strict policy to only use their own in-house catering. But Sidney wanted authentic Caribbean food, so her aunts were cooking instead. Jerk meats, mango salsas, fruit salads, peas and rice, and other popular island food.

The aisle was lined with large bouquets of purple and green

flowers, almost identical to Sidney's bouquet. The only difference was that the flower jewelry in the wedding party's stems were Swarovski crystals and Sidney's were real tear-drop diamonds. An array of green trick dianthus, white anemones, purple peonies, green cymbidium orchids, and purple calla lilies, costing almost three thousand for the bouquet alone.

Sidney looked into her fiancé's teary eyes as she began her vows. "I, Sidney, can't imagine life without you. The whole time I was gone, all I could do was think about you. I haven't had much experience in the love department. You have been my only love. But what I do know is that only a dope boy can love me. You have sacrificed so much and with every breath within me, I will always show you how much I'm grateful.

"Because of you, I laugh, I smile, I dare to dream again.

I look forward with great joy to spending the rest of my

life with you, caring for you, nurturing you, being there for you in all life

has for us, and I vow to be true and faithful for as long as we both shall live."

"I call you 'My Queen' because you are my everything. You are my light, and you've shown me more love than I've ever known. You know me better than anyone else in this world and somehow, still, you manage to love me. You are my best friend and one true love. There is still a part of me today that cannot believe that I'm the one who gets to marry you.

You have been my best friend, mentor, playmate, confidant, and my greatest challenge. But most importantly, you are the love of my life and you make me happier than I could ever imagine and more loved than I ever thought possible... You have made me a better person, as our love for one another is reflected in the way I live my life. So I am truly blessed to be a part of your life, which as of today becomes our life together."

· · ·

Sidney's fiancé finished with forced confidence, as his nerves had the best of him.

The minister, with a smile, announced. "Please join me in introducing Mr. and Mrs. Patrick Young!"

Everyone let out cheers as the newlyweds made their way back down the aisle.

Gucci Mane and Keyshia's reception looked like a homeless shelter compared to the extravagance of Sidney and Patrick's reception. The interior walls were draped with large green and purple shimmering cloth, behind the wedding party table was a large gobo that read "Patrick & Sidney." Birds of paradise and white and purple orchids were placed in three-foot, water-filled vase centerpieces to imitate tropical trees. On the food table, each Caribbean dish was placed on top of large palm leaves. But the real beauty was the cake. A seven-foot cake adorned with purple and green orchids, an edible cake crystal to mimic diamonds, emeralds, and purple sapphires. Each of the seven tiers had a different flavor, with the bottom having the shape of the Jamaican flag when cut into. In total, Bernard spent two million on the reception alone.

All two thousand of the guests were in silence as fifty dancers dressed in green, black and yellow majorette costumes and elaborate carnival headdresses filled into the ballroom. Dancehall music began to play and the dancers came to life as they went into full carnival mode. Everybody was in awe as the fifty dancers moved like one. As quickly as they began, they divided into two groups, creating a walkway. They death dropped to the floor, forming an aisle with their headdresses. The song changed again to "While We're Young," Sidney and Patrick's theme song for the wedding. Patrick and Sidney Emerged dressed in Caribbean Carnival-themed clothing. Sidney wore a provocative and body-forming one piece with a flowing, long, open skirt and purple and green head dress more extravagant than the dancers. She looked like a Caribbean princess as Patrick led her down the aisle of dancers.

The commotion of Sidney and Patrick walking into the reception area had died down and people began to dance and eat.

"Can I have everybody's attention?" I heard Bernard speak from the DJ's booth. But all eyes were on me as the big spotlight landed on me. "Baby, there are many ways to be happy in this life, but all I really need is you. When I look into your eyes, I can see a reflection of the two of us and the life I hope we'll share together. I know my life will never be complete without you beside me to share it. When I look into my heart, I see only you. Keisha Nicole Anderson, will you take a gamble on this old man and be my wife?"

No this nigga didn't. We had only been dating for a short time. But I didn't want to embarrass him in front of his whole family. This spotlight was hot as fuck as everybody waited for my answer. "Bernard, I love you..." I smiled. "You make me so happy..."

🜲 3 🜲

ICE

"Hi man!" I smiled at my son as he sat on the floor of Kimberly's playroom. I thought that she was going to be a bitch or weird like her daughter, but she was actually cool. She didn't give me a hard time about seeing my son. She knew what I did in these streets and she didn't judge me.

"How's Jaya and Israel?" Kimberly asked as she watched me interact with Izzy. "I've noticed she doesn't come with you to pick up and drop off Izzy. She doesn't take my calls anymore."

"Me and Jaya broke up," I commented.

"Because of Trinity?" Kimberly wondered.

I didn't feel comfortable sharing my business, so I kept my answer short. "Something like that."

"Trinity would do anything for her dad. But she learned late that she didn't want to continue to be the obedient daughter. You know the night that Trinity died, I went to her house and I found out some things about my daughter. Things I was willing to go to the grave about. I used to clean up her father's messes, and you see how he is now. I'm not about to do that for Trinity, especially if it hurts others. Trinity was going to make shit right, but she died before that could happen."

Kimberly handed me her phone with a video ready to be watched.

I looked from Kimberly to the phone as Kimberly shrugged. I pressed play and it showed Trinity's house. I could see Trinity mixing some powder into a glass of water before I emerged from the bathroom. I drank the water and it took only a few minutes for me to be slumped on the floor. But what I saw next had me in disbelief. Trap Star and Alisha came out of the back room and helped Trinity drag me up the stairs. I didn't need to see nothing else. My baby mama was so damn crazy. I wished I never met her.

"Trinity sent me this video the day she died. I didn't understand why she would incriminate herself, but I think it was something else going on. Plus, why would she drug you when she was happy with Kevin? My daughter was a lot of things, but this was not her thing."

"I got to go." I put Izzy's bag over my shoulder. Trinity was a dumb bitch and I didn't like how her mama was making excuses. I knew I was drugged and now I had the proof. Not only that, it gave me the proof that Jayson had set up his own granddaughter to be kidnapped.

"There's one more thing, Isaiah." Kimberly's voice shook.

"Okay..."

"Izzy isn't your son. I found the paperwork. The real one. He's Tyler's son."

"Tyler? Tyler Richardson?" I needed to sit down as I stared at the paternity paper with the official seal of the state of Florida, unlike the one that was sent to me in the mail. All this time I'd been taking care of baby that wasn't mine. So much shit could have gone better if Trinity would have kept it one hundred with me. She knew that baby wasn't mine from the get go. I knew I wasn't tripping. I strapped up every time.

"He was Trinity's boyfriend."

"Wait." I had to get this shit clear. "Trap Star is Isaiah Green Junior's father? Jaya's ex-husband?"

"Trinity was obsessed about Jaya. She, for the longest, was jealous of her. I think she sought him out just like she sought you out. Like I said, toward the end of her life, she was trying to do better. I had no clue that Tyler even knew Jaya until I saw his face on the news as the suspect in Israel's disappearance."

"This whole time I thought I was tripping when I would say they look alike. They got the same daddy." I didn't think I could take another revelation.

"I'm sorry. And I understand if you don't want to continue to be in Izzy's life."

"I—" I looked down at the paper again. "It's not Izzy's fault. And he's still going to be my son."

"Ok." Kimberly patted my shoulder. "I'm here for whatever you need."

"Appreciate it," I replied as I prepared to leave.

My mind was all over the place. I didn't know how shit had gone from bad to worse. When Trinity first told me she was pregnant, I was hoping that Izzy was not mine. And now I was hurt that he wasn't mine. But now I knew that I wasn't tripping about not fucking Trinity. Even though Trinity tried to right her wrongs in the end, she had caused so much damage. She knew damn well that Izzy wasn't my baby, hence the fake paternity test results that were sent to me.

As I looked back, I didn't approach Trinity, she approached me. She said all the right things. Liked all the shit I liked. She wanted us to be together and I was with it. But what she didn't know was that once Jaya came back, no bitch was going to hold my attention. But what I didn't know was why some nigga was so worried about me. He couldn't be just tripping on me about me taking over his blocks. He was making major bread, probably more than me.

More than anything, I was happy that I had the evidence to prove to Jaya that I wasn't fucking her sister. I just hoped Jaya would believe me. These last few weeks were hard. I ain't had a home-cooked meal or no pussy. I wanted my family back.

I called Jaya and she answered on the second ring. "Where you at?" I was anxious.

"I'm at home. Why?"

The shit that bothered me the most was Jaya's level of unbothered. That first day she found out about Trinity, she fucked up my truck. But after that, she didn't trip. She let me come get Israel, she didn't cuss me out, she was even cordial, like I was someone she never wanted.

"I need to come holla at you."

"Not today, Isaiah."

"You got a nigga over there or something?"

"Actually, I do."

"You got a nigga around my daughter?" I jumped off the freeway to Jaya's house.

"Isaiah, I thought we already talked about this. I'm doing me. You're doing you. Look, I got to go, I got company and I don't want to be rude. You can come get Israel later if you want to."

"Alright." I tried to hide my anger. "I'll call you later."

"Okay, bet." Jaya hung up her phone.

I was doing ninety to get to her. As soon as pulled up, I saw the second car in her driveway, and I was hot. I got Izzy out the car and used my free hand to bang on the door.

"Ice? The fuck?" Jaya swung open the door. "And you brought Izzy? What the hell is wrong with you?"

"Where he at?" I bypassed Jaya to find some man in the living room, papers on the table, and Israel in the swing.

"How you doing, man?" The man stood up.

"Did Jaya tell you she had a man?" I knew I didn't look like a threat holding a baby, but I had no problem sliding this nigga.

"We are not together!" Jaya shouted. "You can't just come in my house trying to run shit."

"Jay, I'm gonna go." The man looked from me to Jaya.

"Jay?" I looked at this nigga crazy. His ass was being too comfortable.

"Okay, I'll call you later," Jaya replied as the man walked to the door.

"What the fuck, Jaya?"

"Ice, you can't be cheating and then be mad I'm doing me too."

I didn't like Jaya being so calm. It let me know that maybe I had lost her. "I didn't cheat, Jaya."

"I don't want to hear that shit again."

"Trinity drugged me." I showed Jaya my phone.

"Trap Star was there? But why?" Jaya looked confused.

"He's Izzy's daddy."

"But we got the paternity results in the mail." Jaya took Izzy out of my arms. "Why would Trinity lie?"

"At one point, she wanted to be you. But I really think that the person that died really changed for the better. She just was doing the most before."

"This shit is crazy. So you wasn't cheating?" Jaya looked at me. "And Izzy is only my nephew?"

"Yeah." I kissed Jaya lightly.

"I don't know what to say." Jaya looked into my eyes.

"Say that you going to come home."

"I can't keep letting some man come in and save the day. All my life. Shawnie. Trap Star. You. I never had to look out for myself. Shit, I dropped out of high school to be the plug's wife. I love you, but I got to choose me this time, Ice."

"All this shit we been through—" I was so confused.

"I'm not saying I don't want to be with you. I'm saying that I'm not moving out my house. I need to do this for me and Israel."

I didn't want to hear that. I had fought so hard to be in Jaya's life. I wanted us all under one roof. But I was just happy that Jaya was willing to give me another chance. "That's not what I wanted to hear. But I'm on whatever you on."

Jaya smiled. "See, this is why I love you so much."

"Can I ask you a favor though?"

"What's up?"

"Can I get a home-cooked meal and some pussy?"

Jaya laughed. "I got you. Let me put these babies down for a nap."

"I got them." I took Izzy out her hands and went to go pick up Israel. It took me over an hour for me to get them both asleep, but when I emerged from Israel's bedroom, Jaya had the house smelling good with some smothered hamburgers, mashed potatoes, green beans, cornbread, and baked macaroni and cheese. That shit looked good, but not as good as the way Jaya was looking. I grabbed my plate and put it in the microwave.

"You not going to eat?" Jaya questioned as she watched me.

"That's for later." I walked up on her and slid the straps of her tank top down off her shoulders, replacing them with soft kisses.

The nigga in me wanted to rip off her shorts and flip her over and tear that ass up. But the man in me wanted to experience her body like an aged bottle of wine. Jaya didn't speak as I pulled her shirt from over her head. Her skin was so soft, I couldn't get over that shit. God knew what he was doing when he made this one. Because it just wasn't Jaya's looks. It was the person. Her heart, the way she made me laugh. There was nothing like it in this world.

The heat between us was electrifying as my mouth found Jaya's mouth. And as soon as my hands touched her body, I couldn't stop myself as my hands cupped onto Jaya's ass.

I lifted her up around my waist and brought her to the couch. Jaya pushed me back and fell back onto the couch as she kissed me on my neck. I allowed Jaya to be the aggressor as she unbuckled my pants and slid down her shorts.

I almost drowned in the pool of her nectar as I stroked deep and slow. Jaya began to moan like a banshee. I was seeing why I couldn't get Jaya off my mind, because the way she wailed my name and bounced on my dick had me falling in love even more.

Jaya was knocked out on the couch as I lit into my food. Shit was almost as fire as Jaya's pussy. This was what I needed. I was seeing that home wasn't a place. But rather a person. Jaya was home, and as of right now, I was going to accept that she wanted to live on her own. But I didn't think I could last long without her.

Beep.

Jaya's phone was on the counter of the kitchen letting me know she had gotten a text message. I wasn't the type of nigga that went through my bitch's phone. But when I saw the name Ace flash across the screen, I grabbed the phone.

Ace: My bad. I was in the shower. I got you, always. But I'll slide thru tomorrow. I hope you like seafood.

But it was the thread from the day that had me wondering if Jay was moving on.

Jaya: My bad about baby daddy.

Ace: If I had someone like you, I would be tripping too. LOL. We didn't even get to finish.

Jaya: I know. I really do appreciate everything you're doing.

🪷 4 🪷
TIA

"Wow, look who finally comes and sees me."

I rolled my eyes and sat down.

"You still fine as fuck, T." Jayson admired what he saw in front of him.

"Back off of Isaiah, Jayson. You know I ain't fucking with you. Shit been over between us."

"You think I'm tripping about some pussy I ain't had in over twenty years? Let's talk about the fact that you had me thinking Isaiah was my son."

"I told you from the get go that I didn't know if you or Alejandro was the father."

I had so many secrets. For one, I been knowing Jayson for a long time. I met him in Cuba when I was fifteen and he was twenty, and let this nigga game me. I was so in love that we got married after two months. Jayson isolated me by moving me out of Havana where my parents were to across the island to Santiago de Cuba. I was fifteen years old getting my ass whopped. I was making excuses for a sociopath that didn't give a fuck about me.

I was hiding the black eyes from my parents when I would visit them. I made it seem like Jayson was the love of my life, because that's what I felt. One night, I was at the bar and I got too drunk and ended up sleeping with this Cuban man. I didn't tell Jayson about the Cuban man until my belly started to grow. I laid up in the hospital for over a week. My eye was swollen shut and I had two broken ribs. I lied and said I got robbed. When I watched Jayson cry real tears to the policia about how sad he was that his pregnant wife got robbed, I knew that I was married to the devil.

But every time I tried to leave, Jayson would say that I gave up on him like everybody else did. And my naïve ass would go back. I didn't see the wrong until I moved back to the US, pregnant and thinking that the move would make shit better for me and my husband.

I was hoping that my first born was his. But when Isaiah came out light and didn't darken up like Jayson and me, he beat my ass. He hit me so hard that I dropped Isaiah. And Jayson hit me harder for dropping Isaiah. Blaming me for taking his chance away for being a father. I didn't learn until Isaiah was one years old that he divorced Kimberly only two days before we got married and that he already had Trinity.

I was so scared of Jayson that I sent a letter, along with the divorce decree, to him so that I could be free. I moved on with my life, hoping to never lay eyes on Jayson again. But when Isaiah told me that he was dealing with Shawnie's uncle, and then I found out it was Jayson, I was pissed. I didn't even tell Isaiah that I knew Jayson. I knew it would cause so many issues. When I found out that Trinity was Jayson's daughter, I knew it would bring nothing but turmoil to my only son. That's why I gave him the green light to kill the bitch if shit went left. I didn't feel the same about Jaya because she wasn't like Trinity and Jayson. Even though that was her father, I knew that Jaya wasn't grimy.

I wanted to protect my son as much as possible. That's why I told Isaiah that I would handle it. For one, I knew how calculating Jayson was, and I didn't want Isaiah to know my connection to Jayson.

"You wouldn't be no fucking plug if it wasn't for me. I'm sitting here because of you. This ain't about no pussy. This is purely revenge. Bando is a dead nigga."

"Revenge? You killed his dad. You killed that woman. And those are the murders they know about. What about Kimberly's dad? And no telling who else. You are the reason why you are here."

"His daddy killed Maya, T!"

"Ashton killed Jaya's mama?" I referred to Bando's dad. I didn't know that. I changed my number and any letter that came to my house, I never opened. When I said I was done with Jayson, I meant that shit. By the time Isaiah was two years old, I had broken free of Jayson's abuse. Before he went to prison, I heard he had another child, but I was long gone, living my life.

"Yeah. Look, I know I was a horrible husband. I'm sorry. I was young and stupid. But this ain't about us no more. I didn't want Ice fucking with my daughter because I thought he was working with Bando. But I learned that's not true. Bando had my granddaughter kidnapped. He killed my daughter and he's been hitting all Ice's spots. I need you to do this for me, T."

"You know I can't." I looked at Jayson like he'd lost his mind. He really was crazy. When I found out that Jayson was cheating on me with Jaya's mama, I broke up with him. Miami was so small and I only learned about Jaya being Jayson's daughter in the last year. I knew that she had a father that was doing time, but I didn't look into it. I wished I would have. "I will deal with Bando myself. Just leave my son the fuck alone."

"I don't think I can do that, T. I been fronting him hella bread. Bando been hitting all his spots."

I grabbed my head in frustration. I had no idea that shit was this bad. And I was hurt that Isaiah couldn't come to me with the truth, rather than blaming Jayson.

"You know you still got feelings for me. But you got to stop thinking I'm the enemy."

"Nigga, I ain't Maya or Kimberly. And I'm definitely not that scary ass bitch you was beating on in Cuba." I referred to the girl I used to be.

Jayson smiled. "You miss me? You know you will always be the love of my life. Isaiah really should have been mine."

"Well, he's not. You ain't going to like what I do if you keep this shit up. You hurting your daughter too by getting into it with Bando. This shit is all your fault. If some shit happens to my son, you already know—"

"Fuck Bando. I tried to come to an understanding. I killed his dad because he killed my baby mama. Ashton took Maya away from my daughter. Bando don't want no truce. And I don't give a fuck about my life, but my daughters is all I got. He already took Trinity, I can't lose Jaya. He put the hit out for my daughter and cried at her funeral. You think I give a fuck about your threats? You know me better than that."

I knew that Jayson was capable of a lot of shit, but I wished he and Bando would leave Isaiah out of it. I didn't give a fuck who these niggas killed. They weren't going to continue to fuck with mine.

"You've been warned." I stood to leave.

"What's the saying, T? If they can't get to you they will go after your baby. You took over my blocks. Didn't send me a dime from my own dope. Took the chance from me to have a son, and you broke my heart. It's only fair that you help me."

I fucking lost it as I dove over the metal table to hit Jayson. I was no longer the scary bitch, and I had hands. All the pain he brought me, had resurfaced. But Jayson didn't even swing back. Even when the guards came over to restrain me, I was trying to kill this nigga.

"I miss you too, Tia." Jayson lifted my chin. "But you we past talking to Bando. You going have to choose between your baby brother and your son."

"Nigga, fuck your heart. I'm not helping with shit. Stop contacting my son!" I yelled as the guards held my arms.

Jayson laughed. "Bring it, T. I will be seeing you real soon. You know you miss how I used to pipe you down. You never forget your first." Jayson kissed my lips. "I love you. Give me a few weeks and I'ma come holla at you."

I was so stunned from Jayson's calmness that I couldn't move. I was scared for my baby. This wasn't even his battle, and somehow my refusal to not get involved with my ex-husband and my baby brother's beef had Isaiah stuck in the crosshairs.

Jayson looked at me one more time and smiled before walking back to his cell.

"Stay the fuck away from my son!" I screamed at Jayson's back.

"Don't worry, T. I'm coming for Bando. Little brother or not," Jayson said over his shoulder.

5

ACE

ONE YEAR EARLIER

"Here comes this bitch with the bullshit," Bando whispered to me.

"Fall back, my nigga."

"You better get shit right. I don't mind killing this bitch."

"Alright, chill."

"Ace?"

"Yeah?" I let Bando fade into the abyss of my mind.

"How are you?"

"I'm good." I sat down on the couch.

"Let's talk about your parents," my therapist, Monica, spoke as she stared at me.

"There's nothing to talk about. My mom is dead. She died of a broken heart only three months after I got here. My dad was killed," I nonchalantly spoke.

"Do you want to talk about your sister?"

"Fuck her. She helped get me committed."

"You do realize that you killed someone."

"And? The nigga was putting his hands on me and my mother."

"Your mom's boyfriend?"

I looked at Monica like she was stupid. I'd been sitting in a mental hospital for the last fifteen years, since I was thirteen. These muthafuckas kept throwing around words like "bipolar," "mentally unstable," and "sociopath". But what did they expect? I was only five years old when Tia up and left me and my mom to be with Jayson. Me and Tia had the same mama but different daddies. With her dad dead and my dad moving to the US, my mom got a new boyfriend. He used to beat me and my mama's ass. Until one day I got hold of his gun. My mom let Tia paint the picture of me being crazy so that I wouldn't go to jail, but a mental hospital wasn't better. If I wasn't crazy before, I sure the fuck was now.

I didn't hate my sister, but I didn't appreciate her abandoning me for some nigga. The same nigga that killed my dad. Nigga was about to feel my wrath. And not just him, everybody he loved. He took Tia away when I needed her the most, and he took my father's life.

"How does that make you feel, Ace? Your parents?"

"I'm sad. But I have learned to move on," I lied.

"And what about Bando? How does he feel? " Monica spoke about my split personality.

"He was abandoned by everybody that was supposed to love him. And while he was a big part of my healing, he no longer exists." I put on my best performance.

"That's great! And you been taking your medication?"

"Yes, of course. It's the only segway to a better life." I had been sitting in a mental institution for a long time and had learned to play the role. If I would have told Monica that Bando wanted to kill her, she wasn't going to let me out. "I really think that I'm at the point to make changes. I am angry, but I feel that therapy is helping me cope. To channel my anger into something positive." I held up my journal.

"You are using the journal I gave you?" Monica smiled hard.

"You may think I'm not listening, but I am." I faked bashfulness.

I watched with eagerness as Monica began to write in my file. *I recommend early release.*

I just smiled as I saw the words clear as day. Little did Monica know, was that as soon as I was free, I was coming for Jayson. He had no clue what I had in store for him and anybody that ever knew him, including Tia. Ace was chill, but Bando was out for blood.

𝕏 6 𝕏

TIA

CURRENT DAY

"We need to talk."

"There ain't shit to talk about, Tia."

"Oh, nigga, there is a lot to talk about. Where you at?" I didn't have time for this back and forth.

"I'm at my house."

I had nothing else to say as hung up the phone and sped down I-95. I just left seeing my ex-husband, and now I was on my way to see my little brother. I'd been trying for forever to rid myself of Jayson. But now my son was in love with his daughter. I fucked with Jaya, but her daddy was a different story. I knew Isaiah thought I was taking my time by trying to fix the shit with Jayson. But he had no clue that the last time I saw Jayson, he had whopped my ass in front of my son. Isaiah didn't remember because he was only two years old. But I knew that my ass was laid up in the bed for a week trying to mend a black eye and a broken heart.

And shit didn't help that there was still a small part of me that loved him. That missed him. He was my first everything. He was my first love, my first boyfriend. I had to remember that he was also my first abuser, the first man I was scared of, and the first man to break my heart. That small inkling of love had nothing on my love for my first born. When it came to Isaiah, fuck Jayson.

"What the fuck I do now?" My little brother Ace looked at me, annoyed, when I pulled up to his house.

"You been hitting all my son's spots, nigga!" I shoved Ace back as I got out of the car. "And why the fuck you didn't tell me that your dad killed Maya?"

"I didn't think the shit was relevant. My beef ain't with Isaiah. My beef is with Jayson."

I looked at the younger version of me. The child that had my mother's cocoa-hued skin. The child that had my eyes. The child my mother had on my father. The child that grew up without a sister. My brother who came looking for me six months ago. This beef that Isaiah was having with Jayson had me not aware that Ace was involved too. And not only that, he happened to be my brother. I knew that Jayson and Isaiah were going to war, but this whole time, it was Ace hitting Isaiah's spots. And now my ass was going to have to rectify all this masculine, toxic bullshit.

I ain't going to lie, I had turned my back on my baby brother. But not on purpose. I was getting my muffin cap pulled back blue by Jayson and raising my son. I was broken back then and I got so caught up worrying only about Tia, Isaiah, and Jayson, that I wasn't visiting Ace and my mom. I had no clue what my mom's boyfriend was doing to them. When I moved to the US, I didn't look back. After Ace killed our mom's boyfriend, I paid top dollar for my baby brother to go to a mental hospital rather than jail. And while I failed in going to see him, I made sure them crazy house bills were paid in full and on time.

"Well, you got my son in the middle of it."

"I didn't know he was your son, Tia. You should have said, 'bro, this nigga Ice is your nephew.'"

"I didn't even know you was selling drugs. Just fall back on Isaiah." I was trying to dead this shit.

"You didn't answer the question. Why haven't you introduced me to my nieces and nephew?"

"It's complicated."

"Because I was in a crazy house? You embarrassed of me?"

I was. I didn't want anybody to know that my brother was crazy. As far as everybody was concerned, I didn't even have a brother. I knew I was wrong to turn my back on Ace, especially after our mom died. But he was in that mental institution talking to himself, paranoid, and flipping out. How was I going to bring my kids around that? To be honest, Ace wasn't supposed to get out. He was fucking bat shit crazy. He killed before and he would continue to kill again.

"I'm not embarrassed. I just don't want to confuse my kids. Just back off of Isaiah."

"And if I don't?" Ace towered over me, his eyes heating up like he was possessed.

When it came to my kids, I would go toe to toe with any fucking body. I quickly grabbed the gun that was hidden in my bra strap from the back. I didn't point it at my brother, but I took the safety off.

"Before you blink, you going to be on the ground. Ace, live your life. Do whatever you want to do. But you keep my kids out of your bullshit. This is the last time I'm going to speak on it. Keep fucking with me, and you going see Mama quicker than you think."

✣ 7 ✣

ICE

"Finish what?" I shoved Jaya's phone in her face, waking her up.

"Ice, move," Jaya grumbled as she tried to turn her back to me.

"So that's what we're doing? Hopping from dick to dick?"

Jaya finally opened her eyes. "What?"

"We been broken up for only a few weeks and you already fucking somebody else?"

"And if I was? We wasn't together." Jaya sat up.

"So you fucking this nigga around my daughter?"

"Who?"

"The nigga that was here!" I didn't know why she was playing stupid.

Jaya quickly glanced at the text message thread I had open on her phone. "You went through my phone?"

"Is you fucking him?" I didn't care about how I got the information.

"No!"

"So why is he talking about finishing? Finishing what?"

"He's helping me get my real estate license. He was helping

me study." Jaya got up and showed me the papers sitting on the coffee table. "See?"

Ring, Ring

Jaya's phone began to ring, and it was that nigga Ace calling. I hurried up and answered the phone.

"I got a meeting that runs late. Can we meet tomorrow around seven—"

"This ain't Jaya," I replied as Jaya rolled her eyes as I put the phone on speaker.

Ace started to laugh. "You pressed, nigga?"

"Nigga, it's whatever. Shit, pull up." I got angry. This bitch ass nigga was going to have to see me.

"The fuck?" Jaya snatched her phone out of my hand. "Yes, seven works," Jaya responded quickly before hanging up.

"So you about to play in my face with this nigga? Yup. Bet."

"He helped me get this place and now he's helping me get my license. He's not trying to fuck me. And I'm not trying to fuck him."

"You wouldn't need a place if you would come back home. I don't trust that nigga."

"Why, because he's a man? I'm not you. I don't be entertaining bitches."

"When? I know you ain't talking about Trinity!"

"No, I'm talking about me! You was with Trinity and what do you do, cheat on her with me. Broke up with her the next day."

"Do you hear yourself? I'm a nigga. I know how niggas move. He wants to fuck—"

"Well, I don't want to fuck him and he hasn't come at me like that. You want me to trust you, and I want you to trust me too." Jaya stepped in my space. "So what you about to do?"

"You got some dick and now you kicking me out?"

"Pretty much." Jaya stepped back with her hand on her hip.

"Bet." Jaya wanted to do her, I wasn't going to keep chasing her.

"I'm just playing!" Jaya laughed as she brought me closer.

"That shit wasn't funny, bruh."

"You going to spend the night or what?"

"I don't like how you moving, Jay." It was like Jaya had evolved into another person. She was starting to act like a nigga and to be honest, I didn't like that shit. Her level of unbothered was bothering the fuck out of me.

"Why? Because I'm not little naïve Jaya? You, Trinity, Trap Star, and my dad are the reason for that. I had to stop depending on muthafuckas for everything and do shit myself. I'll always be grateful for Shawnie allowing me to work at the food truck, but I got to get to my own bag."

"And what about me?" I was feeling some type of way. Niggas didn't understand how much I would pay to go back to the night I proposed to Jaya. We were so happy, we had our daughter, we had our family. I didn't want Jaya feeling naïve or none of that shit. But I was a man and I wanted to provide for my family. Jaya didn't have to work if she didn't want to. Her ass was thinking like she was a single mama with a sorry ass baby daddy, and that wasn't the case. Shit, her ass didn't even have to live in this small ass duplex. I bought us a big ass six-bedroom home down in South Miami. She had my baby in Walmart clothes when I could have Israel rocking baby Fendi. I wasn't understanding why Jaya was wanting to live in gutter when I could have her in luxury.

"What about you?" Jaya stared at me with cold eyes.

"You tell me. Have you seen this muthafucka? There is barely anything in here. And why the fuck my daughter wearing a six-dollar outfit from Walmart?"

"But it's mine! It's my hard work."

I needed to regroup my words. "I'm not knocking you for taking care of yourself. I'm saying as your man, as the father of your child, how can I, as a man, be okay with you living like this?"

"You act like I'm sleeping on an air mattress at Shawnie's house—"

"I had a problem with that shit, and so that's why I moved

you into the townhouse." I hated the fact that Trap Star was Jaya's first boyfriend. Because he had her thinking niggas were supposed to be okay if they bitch was doing bad.

"But you act like I'm out here struggling just because I'm not living the way you living. I'm happy, Ice."

"Happy without me?" I laid the cards on the table.

"Why do you have to make this about you?"

"Answer the question. Are you happy without me?"

"I miss you. I love you. And I'm happy that I can take care of myself for a change."

"So you want me to go?" Nigga was all in his feelings. Jaya been hollering I had been the love of her life. That I was bae, but as soon as this bitch get her own Rent-A-Center couch it's fuck Ice? All the shit we went through. And none of that shit was my fault. I ain't never cheated on Jaya. Her dad and her weird ass sister were making my life a living hell, and I still chose her. I still loved her. I fought through all the bullshit for us to be together, and now I was being treated like a nothing-ass nigga.

Jaya placed her hands on my chest and stared up into my eyes. "No, I don't want you to go. But I want you to understand that the men in my life have been taking care of me for so long that I became too dependent. We were moving too fast, Isaiah. Here I am freshly broken up with my husband, pregnant, homeless, and I ain't even back home for a month and we jump into a relationship. You break up with my sister and we just think shit supposed to go good? You see the shit we been through?"

"So what, we ain't engaged anymore? We ain't together?"

"We are together. But we need to hold off on the engagement part."

"Damn." It was taking everything in me not to shed a fucking tear. "I got some shit I got to handle. I'll holler at you."

Jaya grabbed my arm. "Baby, don't go. I'm not saying that we can't get engaged, but can we start over? Can we do it right this time?"

"We got a whole daughter. Start what over?" I wasn't understanding the logic.

"Like date. I need to heal, Ice. I never got to grieve my marriage."

"Your marriage? The fuck!"

"I don't miss Trap Star, but I need to heal from that shit. I need to heal from my daughter being kidnapped. I need to heal from my sister's death. I need to heal from my toxic relationship with my dad. I been through a lot in a short amount of time—"

"I'm not saying you haven't. But damn, Jay, you act like a nigga ain't been here through all that! Do you understand what the fuck I got to go through in these streets? Huh? You think I want to go to your dad for help? I'm tried as a man every fucking day, yo! The only peace I have is you and my kids. And you want to take that from me? What, because I'm a man, I ain't got feelings? Do you think I like waking up every day without you by my side? I been in love with you since the moment I laid eyes on you. I ain't Shawnie, I'm not entertaining the runner-up bitch. I know where my heart is, and it's with you."

"Babe." Jaya kissed me. "Don't do this. Don't make me feel guilty for wanting to be a better person."

"Alright, man." I relinquished.

Jaya began to smile. "Thank you." Jaya began to kiss on me. Her voodoo ass had me. I was about to go with this Ms. Independent bullshit.

Jaya grabbed me by the hand and led me to her bedroom. It didn't help that her ass was all naked, looking good and shit. Motherhood had changed her body for the better. She was thick, and even them tiger stripes on her abdomen were sexy as fuck.

"You keep giving me this fire ass pussy and then wonder why a nigga be tripping," I spoke honestly.

"It's fire because it only belongs to you." Jaya caressed my dick. "I'm forever yours, Isaiah." Jaya maneuvered so that she could be on her back and I could fall into the pussy.

I woke the next morning hearing Jaya singing from the kitchen, and bacon attacking my nostrils. I slipped on my boxers, rinsed my mouth out with some mouthwash, and walked into the kitchen.

I stood back and watched Jaya move as she had Izzy and Israel in the high chairs, feeding them and singing to them. The fact that Jaya never did or said anything bad about Izzy, spoke volumes. She really had a good heart. I didn't want to leave. Hell, I didn't want to be in my bed by myself tonight. Wherever Jaya went, she made a house into a home. She was my rib, and I didn't know how I was going to function. But I loved Jaya enough to give her the space to grow as a woman.

"Good morning." Jaya continued to feed the babies.

"Good—" I started, but my phone began to ring.

"Why ain't Jaya answering the phone?" Shawnie got loud.

Shawnie really had a problem with thinking that niggas were under him, especially when he was angry.

"Take that bass out your—"

"Dejah is being rushed into surgery. Tell Jaya to come to Jackson Memorial." Shawnie hung up the phone.

Once I told Jaya what was going on, she headed to the hospital and I took the kids to my mom's. By the time I got to the hospital, Jaya, Dejah's mom, Shawnie, and Keisha were in the waiting room.

"What is Keisha doing here?" I questioned Jaya as I pulled her aside.

"That's a good question. I'm just trying to keep the peace. So I told Dejah's mom that she was my lesbian friend," Jaya whispered as we both looked at Keisha. I guess Keisha could pass for a lesbian since she was wearing sweats, a sports bra, no makeup, and some jailhouse braids. She was giving me "Cleo" from *Set it Off* vibes.

"How you invite your ex-girlfriend to the hospital and your

wife and daughter are fighting for their lives? Cousin or not, Shawnie knows he's wrong for this one."

It was none of my business how this nigga was moving, so I kept my answer short. "Shit is crazy."

"Family of Dejahnae Mitchell?" The doctor came out of nowhere. "Good news. Both mom and baby are just fine. We were able to stop the contractions. It seems like Dejahnae had a bladder infection due to not drinking enough water. The lack of water decreased the amniotic fluid, causing early labor. We are going to keep her overnight so that we can get her fluids back up."

It was like the tension had dispersed now that everyone knew that Dejah and the baby were okay.

"Can I see her?" Shawnie asked, and before the doctor could say yes or no, Shawnie was making his way back to the hospital rooms.

It seemed like as soon as it was known that Dejah was okay, Dejah's mom started to be messy. "Were you and my daughter scissoring?" Miss Tomika questioned Keisha.

"What is scissoring?" Keisha wondered.

"You know...when two women go to pound town without the pickle."

"Hold up, you think I'm fucking Dejah?" Keisha looked at Miss Tomika.

"Well, are you?"

Keisha began to laugh. "If I was a lesbian, you think I would mess with your basic, dumb ass daughter? No. I would get me a manly one like Young MA."

"So who are you?"

If was like the air had left the room as Keisha's face dripped in sarcasm. "I'm Shawnie's ex. The one that he can't get over."

I heard Jaya whisper fuck, and shit went left after that. Miss Tomika went to swing on Keisha, but not before Keisha swung back. I moved fast to get in between the two women. But as soon as I did that, Miss Tomika had turned her anger onto

Shawnie, who had stepped back into the waiting room. She wasn't dumb enough to put her hands on him, but she did speak her mind.

"My daughter was fighting for her life and you got—"

"It was a bladder infection," Shawnie countered.

"It don't matter! We just found that out. I don't give a damn if it was a hang nail! You are not about to disrespect my daughter by having your ex here."

"Me and her ain't fucking. Keisha is going to always be here for me though. I—"

"I'ma just leave," Keisha said from the side of Shawnie.

"Nah, Zo. Stay. Fuck her." Shawnie grabbed Keisha by the arm and marched her to the other side of the waiting room.

Jaya, Ms. Tomika, and I watched in shock as Keisha and Shawnie argued about her staying. Shawnie was moving foul with this one. His wife was laid up in a hospital bed and he was damn near begging his ex not to leave. I thought we all knew it, Dejah and Shawnie weren't going to last forever. Not when his heart lived in human form, aka Keisha.

"I caught that nigga slipping. He in a body bag right now," the text message from Carlise read.

"Who?"

"Bando."

8

JAYA

"You muthafuckas are so damn messy," I commented as Israel and Izzy sat on the floor of my house.

"I didn't do shit. Girl, I was minding my own business when I called Shawnie to let him know that..."

I let my head drop and shook it from left to right.

"Okay, I called to see how he was doing and he told me he was at the hospital. Bitch, to be honest, I thought it was your ass that was sick."

"And what about this?" I lifted up Keisha's hand so she could realize that she was engaged to Mr. Otis.

"I could see if I was cheating. I'm not. I was just checking on him, damn."

"Bitch, you about to be causing problems in their marriage." I recalled how Shawnie was more worried about Keisha leaving than Dejah's health.

"I'm not about to be doing shit. Girl, I wasn't the side chick before he was married. I'm not about to be now. I got a good man that loves me."

"But do you love him?"

"You worried about the wrong shit, sis."

"Answer the question."

"Not everybody can be with their soulmate like you, Jay. I'm doing what makes me happy."

"Y'all are so damn stubborn. Neither one of y'all are happy. You and Shawnie playing with these people's hearts. And we both know that Viagra and heartbreak going to end up killing Mr. Otis. Girl, quit playing with that man."

"How many times I got to tell you his name Bernard? You get on my damn nerves. Don't hate that my man is mature."

"Girl, nobody jealous of you being with that old man but Mother Jenkins from church."

"What the fuck ever. Girl, I don't know what the hell is going on with Shawnie."

"You," I stated the obvious. "He's not happy, Kesh. You know how he feels about you."

"That's no longer my concern. If he wanted me, he wouldn't have married Dejah. Real talk. Shawnie already know I don't do that second choice shit. We are always going to have a connection. I was supposed to be his first everything. Yeah, we smashed for the first time and all that kiddy shit, but who did he marry? Who he give his first child to? Not me. So, I'm good."

I just sat there and stared at Keisha as she tried to convince me that she was over Shawnie. I didn't know who she thought was fooling, but it wasn't me. I didn't want Keisha to come in and break-up Shawnie and Dejah, but I knew my cousin wasn't happy. Hopefully, everything worked out for all of them. But somebody's feelings were going to be hurt.

Ding dong

I heard my doorbell ring. I wasn't expecting company, as Keisha and I shared a confused look.

"Ace?" I opened the door to see my friend standing there.

"You forgot?"

Then it dawned on me that Ace was coming to help me with the real estate exam. I was happy for him to help. I would only be lying to myself, but I was attracted to Ace's fine ass. But I wasn't about to hop from dick to dick. But I certainly needed to be thinking about studying rather than the visible bulge in Ace's jeans.

"Aww shit, I did." I hit myself in the head.

"We can always hook up another—"

"Nah, right now is okay." I stepped to the side to let Ace in the house.

"Bitch, you are so messy." Keisha stared at me as her eyes shifted to Ace. "How you doing, Ace?"

"Keisha, how's everything going?" Ace sat on the floor with my babies. Even though Izzy was my biological nephew, he was more like my son. Shit, I think I had him more than Kimberly and Ice. He was even getting to the point that when I would leave he would cry. He didn't know no better. He didn't have a mama no more and I was the closest thing to one. I planned on telling Izzy the truth of me being his auntie later in life. But right now, he needed someone to love him like a mother.

"I'm Gucci. Thank you for hooking up my girl with this place. So, what's up with you and Jaya? Y'all fucking or what?"

My head turned so fast that I thought it would snap off. "Just ignore her." I rolled my eyes as I grabbed my exam papers from my newly purchased dining room table, aka a card table from Walmart.

"Don't ignore me, Ace. You knocking down my best friend?"

Ace chuckled. "No, Jaya is my friend." Ace smiled as he looked at me.

Yup, the feelings were mutual, we were feeling each other. However, I had a man. I wasn't going to be the chick that said they were doing them and in all actuality was doing all kind of niggas.

"See?"

"Yeah, ok." Keisha kicked her Air Maxes off.

"What are you doing?" I questioned.

"Chaperoning, bitch. I know your ass too well. Friends don't let friends fuck side niggas."

"You stupid." I forced myself to chuckle, but Keisha was

right. I wanted to fuck Ace and for some reason, I was super horny right about now. I didn't want her to stay, I needed her to stay. "But you being here and helping with the babies until Ice gets here will help me out."

"Ice?" Ace stared at me strangely.

I didn't know why it took so much force to respond that I had a man. "Yes, my boyfriend."

"Aww, okay. The dude that was tripping?"

I rolled my eyes since Ice was over here acting like a dummy. "Yeah, that's him."

"I think he went to school with my nephew. His mama named Tia?"

"Yeah!" Damn, Miami was small. "You know her too?" I was curious.

"No. But I remember her coming up to the school and shit."

"If you want, I can hook y'all up." If he was smashing someone else, maybe it would stop my urge to slide my pussy across his face.

"She looks too much like my sister. I'm good."

"That's crazy you said that shit, because you look a lot like Ms. Tia."

"Whatchu trying to say?" Ace got playful. "All black people look alike?" We all laughed.

"No." I changed the subject. "You ready to study?"

"You making dinner?" Keisha chimed in to me.

"How about I order us some food, what y'all like?" Ace offered.

"I like you, Ace. And dessert too. After the day I had with my ex, I need some Casamigos. Where's your card at?" Keisha questioned.

"What you mean?" I wondered. Because the only living ex she had was Shawnie. Like I said, me and Shawnie didn't have no secrets. Everything he did, I knew about, and vice versa.

"Girl, we got into it at Target."

SIREN

"Wait. You was at Target while his wife was in the hospital?" Shawnie's ass was damn trifling.

"No, bitch. We ran into each other there. He—"

"So why is Shawnie at Target and Dejah—"

"Girl, I don't know. That's your cousin. Now, back to you, Ace. Can we get some liquor and food?" Keisha turned her attention to Ace.

"Money ain't a question. What do y'all want to eat and drink?" Ace smiled.

I knew I was with Ice, and he was certainly bae, but the way Ace was moving, had me feeling some type of way. Keisha had saved me from letting this nigga bend me over the couch, but she wasn't going to be here every time.

Lord help me.

✤ 9 ✤

SHAWNIE

"What's wrong, Shawnie?" Dejah questioned as she laid in the bed watching me move around our bedroom.

I stopped looking through the drawers for some boxers and turned to face my wife. "Nothing. Why you ask that?"

"My mom told me that Keisha was at the hospital. You begged her to stay?"

I didn't want lie to Dejah. "I was stressed about the baby and you. I needed someone to talk to."

"Then get a dog. The shit is disrespectful. I'm feeling like your body is here but your heart is with Keisha."

"I'm tired of you always bringing up Keisha. Like, damn, the only woman I'm fucking is you."

"No!" Dejah got mad. "It's the fact she is always around. She's at your mama's house. She's at your cousin's house. Then! Me and your daughter get sick and you got the audacity to have her at the hospital. Don't make it seem like I am the one making up shit when this bitch is constantly being put in my face."

"You ain't got to call her out her name, Dejah. We got history. She ain't trying to fuck me. She got a whole fiancé. I'm not kicking it with her."

41

"I can't tell. Just because y'all used to fuck around don't mean she has to continue to be around."

"Shit is deeper than that."

"Well, enlighten me, JaShawn."

I stared at Dejah and it felt like it was eons before I spoke. If I told Dejah how deep me and Keisha's soul ties went, it would break her heart. I had killed for Keisha...twice. I was buying school clothes, getting her hair done when we were younger. I was there for her when no one else was there. Shit, when Keisha went to go live with her grandma after her mom died, I was helping pay bills. As long as I had breath in my body, Keisha would never go without. Just like no matter what storm I went through, my solace would always reside with Keisha. So, when my wife and daughter's lives were in danger, I needed my best friend.

"We ain't on no romance shit. We just been through a lot together." I kept my answer truthful but vague.

"I get that. But you married me. I'm carrying your firstborn child. You going to have to let that shit go. How we supposed to make shit work if you got your ex hovering around?"

"What do you want me to do, Dejah? The fuck. I—"

"I want you to tell her to stop hanging out with your mama. Stop being besties with Jaya. You say she got a fiancé, then she needs to be around that man's family and not my husband's!"

"I don't know how you think that shit is about to happen. Jaya fucks with you, but they been friends since kindergarten. My family has made room for you too."

"How? Your mama don't like me! She basically said that you was a dummy for marrying me, knowing that you should have been with Keisha."

I didn't know what to say to that shit. Because Ma Dukes didn't hold her tongue for no damn body. It wasn't that she didn't like Dejah, it was just that she knew that maybe I didn't make the right decision. "My mom does like you." I didn't want to keep this shit going, because all this shit was going to do was hurt Dejah's feelings more. "I'ma get at you later." I quickly located my clothes.

"Holla at me later? The fuck? Do I look like some sneaky link that you just gave forty dollars to? I'm your wife! You—"

Dejah wanted to argue and I was trying to spare her feelings. Her ass was pissing me off and I was bound to say some fucked up shit. She was so worried about Keisha and not taking care of home. I knew she was pregnant, but ever since we got married, I ain't been getting no pussy or no head. And if I did, Dejah would just lay there. Then on top of that, the nagging was too much. No man wanted to be with no bitch that was talking shit and not giving up no pussy. I didn't know how long I was going to last.

I got dressed downstairs in the living room and made my way to work. I was finally off of parole and quit my job at Amazon. I was finally back on my feet as that nigga. And I wasn't risking my freedom to do it. Miami Hustle was bringing in more customers by the day, and my customers loved my Haitian-themed soul food. Life was good, and the only complaint I had was my wife.

ॐ

"Yo, bro, thanks for looking out." Ice slapped hands.

"Bet. You already know I got your back. But nigga, don't end up like me. This drug shit ain't forever." I wasn't trying to tell another man how he lived his life, but Ice was with my cousin and raising my niece. All the heat that he was getting out in these streets from this nigga Bando wasn't good, and I didn't want that smoke to trickle over to Jaya and Israel.

"Nigga, if you worried about Jaya and the baby, just say that." Ice passed me the blunt.

"I don't want no harm coming to my people."

"I know that Jaya is your cousin, but that's my bae. I ain't about to let no nigga touch her or my daughter. I'm making moves to get out this shit now. Have you ever seen a nigga in his seventies selling drugs? That shit don't happen. Either you on a t-shirt or twelve got you locked down for life. I don't want that for me or Jaya."

"So, what's up with this Bando nigga then?" I was curious.

"He dead."

"What you mean dead?"

"Carlise caught that nigga slipping. I saw the body myself."

"Alright." I felt somewhat relieved. "And my uncle?"

"I got to pay that nigga back. But my mom is handling that."

"I didn't even know your mom knew my uncle."

"Shit, me either. But she went to the pen to holler at him. I don't know what she said, but he ain't been on no bullshit. But even with Bando gone, I'm still not trying to sell drugs forever."

"I thought my ass was going to be the plug forever until twelve came and fucked my whole world up. Lost my house, my car, my money, and my bitch."

Ring, ring. I saw my phone ringing, and I could feel a smile growing on my face.

"What's good with you?"

"I need your help." Keisha's voice cracked like she was holding back tears.

My captain save a bitch mode had activated and I was down to do whatever to help her out. "What's wrong?"

"A couple of the girls from the club got invited to do this private party. But these niggas are on some weird shit. I came to dance and that's it. These niggas want to fuck and I ain't with that shit. I locked myself in the back room. You know I can handle shit on my own, but there's like fifteen niggas and I ain't got my heat on me."

"Why didn't you call Mr. Clarence?" I was down to be there for Keisha, but she had a nigga.

"What the fuck he going to do? He ain't about that life. These niggas is drunk and on they Junior's bachelor party shit. They ain't about to let me just walk out this house peacefully.

You know what Tommy did to me. I don't want that to happen again. I'm scared, Shawnie." Keisha softly cried.

"Say less. Send me your location, I'm on my way." Keisha and I ended the call and I saw the notification from Keisha with her location. "I got to go to Hollywood to pick up Keisha. I'ma get at you later." I dapped up Ice before I exited his car.

"Go get wifey, bro," Ice joked.

It usually took twenty-eight minutes to get from Miami to Hollywood, but the way I was driving, I got there in seventeen. I wasn't with Keisha anymore, but if she called I was sliding niggas. I was out of prison when Tommy raped her and I felt bad because I wasn't there to protect her. I was even more mad that this nigga thought he could handle Keisha any way, knowing I would kill him. The shit had me wanting to re-kill his bitch ass.

Just the thought of it had me on one hundred. So when I pulled up to the house off Harbor Court, I was strapped and ready for whatever. I didn't have to kick in the door because the muthafucka was already unlocked. These niggas were slipping. There were naked bitches every fucking where. The music was blasting, but not loud enough to drown out the sex noises. I was all about getting my dick wet, but Keisha's safety was heavily on my mind.

All eyes were on me as I made my way to the living room.

"Yo, bro, I think that you at the wrong spot." Some nigga stopped me by putting his hand on my chest. I looked down at the nigga's hand and then looked him in his eyes.

Oh, this nigga done fucked up, as I whipped my gun out so fast that the barrel was damn near inside his nose.

"Nobody make a fucking move! Keisha! Where is she at?" My eyes became menacing as my attention bounced around the room.

Nobody made a move, and the nigga that was standing in front of me was shaking as I was ready to blow his head off. "I-I...Keisha! Your people out here!" the man yelled out.

"Turn that music off!" I spoke to no one in particular, but at least two niggas scrambled to get to the Bluetooth to turn it off.

Some stripper bitch stood up and tried to address me. "Heiress? I can go get her," she offered.

"Nah. I'm good. Keisha!" I yelled again. I didn't know what was in these rooms, and I had to be able to control the situation.

Keisha emerged wearing a silver thong and matching bra. I was all about a woman getting to the bag, but Keisha needed to understand that some niggas didn't know the difference between a stripper and a prostitute. I wasn't saying that a nigga trying to push up on a woman that didn't want him was cool. But her outfit didn't necessarily say she was a square. Either way, that was bae. And if her ass wore nothing but a smile and some stilettos and said no, her ass meant no.

"Which one of these niggas tried you?" I looked at Keisha as I still held the gun in the man's face.

"I just want to go." Keisha did her best to cover her body with her arms. Now her ass was shy.

"You know I ain't about to do that."

"It's not that—"

"Either you tell me who it is or I'ma start shooting everybody."

"Bro, I just got here."

"Yeah, me too."

A few niggas spoke up.

"Him. Him. And him." Keisha pointed to two dudes on the couch and the man that I had my gun trained on.

My face broke into a grin. "You tried to rape my bitch?"

"See, what happened was—" I didn't need to hear an explanation as I took the butt of the gun and beat that nigga's ass.

"Anybody move and your ass is next," I spoke as soon as the cold metal brushed across dude's face. I done wore my ass out by whooping this nigga's ass, so I chose to shoot the two niggas that were on the couch. They asses was crying from where I shot them in the legs. They bad.

"Where's your cloth—" I asked Keisha once we got on the porch, but she cut me off as she wrapped her arms around me.

"Thank you, Shawnie." Keisha looked up at me with teary eyes. I couldn't resist the heat that dispersed between us. My feelings for Keisha were strong as fuck and I needed to stop playing. I didn't say shit as I leaned down and kissed her lips. Keisha's lips were so soft as I pulled her into me.

"Stop—" Keisha pulled away from me. "I'm not about to do this with you, Shawnie."

"Where did you park?" I backed down. Plus, I knew one of them muthafuckas called the police.

"I rode with one of the dancers. But my shit is at the room."

"Alright, come on. Give me the addy," I told Keisha as we got into my truck.

Once we got to the Hard Rock Hotel, I had other plans on my mind. For one, I didn't want to go home, and two, I wanted to spend some time with Keisha.

"You in a rush to go home?" I questioned as I watched Keisha pack up her bag.

"Why?" Keisha sat on the bed.

"Because I want to chill with you."

"Go home to your wife."

"I made a mistake," I spoke the truth.

"That's not my problem. When I stood in front of your door damn near begging for you to come back, what did you say? *It's over, Zo. I appreciate you for looking out for me, but this shit wouldn't have gotten this bad if you weren't fucking with Tommy.*"

My own words cut me deep. "I know what I said, Keisha. And I'm saying I made a mistake. I should have chose—"

Keisha began to laugh. "Nigga, do I look like the bitch that was going to wait for you? After you done got married, got the bitch pregnant, and told me to go do me? Well, I did. I got a good man who don't play no games about me."

"Then why didn't you call him? Every time shit goes down, you calling me. You act like I don't fucking know you, Zo! You don't love that nigga like you love me. Just like I don't love Dejah like I love you. I kept fighting against my heart. I kept lying to myself that I was over you. But I'm not, Kesh." I pulled Keisha to her feet.

"If you think I'm about to be your side bitch, you got me fucked up."

"Side bitch? The fuck? You are my whole fucking heart. You think I'ma hide that from anybody?"

"What about your—" I knew I was wrong for stepping to Keisha knowing I was married. I knew that I was on some fuck boy shit. But I couldn't continue to live without the one who held my heart. I didn't give a fuck that I was married. I didn't give a fuck that Keisha was engaged to that old ass nigga. I didn't let Keisha finish her sentence as I let my hands fall to the small of Keisha's back as I let my mouth find hers.

I felt Keisha's resistance melt in my arms as she kissed me back with velocity. I wasn't a cocky nigga, but Keisha had been with a total of three men, and Tommy or Mr. Clarence wasn't putting it down like me. And since I been out, I had fucked a lot of bitches, but no bitch could have me nutting like Keisha. We spent so much time learning how to pleasure each other in the past that I didn't know if a woman could hold my attention like Kesh.

I wanted to smash so bad, but I wanted to take my time to savor every moment. I ain't been in between Keisha's legs in a minute, but she was worth the wait. It didn't take long for me to undress Kesh since she only had on the stripper outfit.

I had to step back and admire her chocolate beauty. Every curve. The scar on her leg from when I pushed her down the stairs when we were seven and nine years old. The brightness in her eyes. But it wasn't just the physical. It was the girl I watched turn into a woman. I saw through the thug shit and saw strength born out of pain and the love that I helped mold. I didn't even know why I let my pride get in the way of what we had.

"Why you staring at me like that?" Keisha got shy, covering her breasts up with her hands.

"Now you shy?" I grabbed up Keisha's hands. "You a whole stripper."

"See? Yeah. No." Keisha tried to pull away from me, but I wasn't letting go.

I was prepared to be on my smooth lover shit, but Keisha needed that thug dick. Keisha was butt ass naked as I picked her up and maneuvered her to straddle my face.

Keisha was wet as fuck. Her juices drenched my face like a palm tree in a tropical storm. As soon as my tongue flickered against her chocolate pearl, Keisha let it rain. Her pussy tasted and felt so good as I gripped her thighs tighter as she bucked against my tongue.

"Damn, Shawnie," Keisha whined as I continued to fuck her with my mouth.

Keisha began to grind harder and I knew she was about to nut. I grabbed Keisha by her waist and slammed her down on my face as my tongue attacked her opening like bear trying to get to the honey. Just like that, Keisha's honey pot spilled down my face in feminine nectar.

We were both out of breath as I grabbed up Keisha and flipped her on her back. I tried to dive in the pussy, but her opening was so tight that there was no way I was going plunge in. I smiled to myself because it meant that that Mr. Clarence wasn't putting it down. I placed Keisha's legs up on my shoulders as I inched my way in. Keisha arched her back as she bit down on her lip.

There was pussy, and then there was fire ass pussy. Keisha always had that WAP but somehow, it got better with age. The pussy that I was knocking down in the broom closet when I was in prison had transformed into euphoric paradise.

I barely had four inches in before I felt the urge to nut. I was trying to think of other shit like, can I really save twenty percent on my car insurance if I switched to Geico? Just anything not to go out like a bitch ass nigga. It'd been some years since me and Keisha fucked, and I couldn't be looking like I was pussy whipped. Fuck. I was only seven strokes in and I was nutting. I tried to play the shit off.

"You want some water, babe?"

Keisha sat up laughing like I was a stand-up comedian. "All that shit you was talking and yo' ass couldn't last in the pussy for two minutes! Just like when we lost our virginity."

I felt like Keisha was challenging me, and I wasn't that fifteen-year-old boy anymore. No bitch had me cumming like a punk ass nigga but Keisha.

"The shit is all your fault."

"My fault?" Keisha put her hand on her chest like she was appalled.

"You know you got that fire." I began to kiss Keisha as my dick rocked up like crack.

"Is that right?" She smiled as she let me slip my tongue in her mouth.

I was glad I got that first nut out the way, because I was about to murder the pussy. I ain't going to lie, Keisha's walls were both slippery wet and tight. But her ass wasn't laughing no more as I hit her G-spot repeatedly. Her ass was cumming back to back. But that last one took us both out. I couldn't even describe the shit. Like, sex was one thing, and for me it was like a hand shake, it didn't mean shit. I wasn't tripping over no pussy. But to fuck someone you loved, someone who you could be you with, that was a whole different level.

"I love you, Kesh," I whispered in Keisha's ear as she dozed off in my arms.

"I love you too," Keisha replied as sleep was winning the battle to keep her eyes open.

I laid there for a minute watching my bae sleep. Damn, her ass was beautiful. The Lord knew what he was doing when he made Keisha. He was probably like, this one is for JaShawn. In a sea of pretty bitches, Keisha would always stand out as the most beautiful.

"Dejah?" I dialed my wife.

"Baby, you alright? I was worried about you—"

"I'm not coming back, Dejah," I stated facts.

"What?" I could hear the hurt in her voice.

"I got to apologize. I really wanted shit to work out with us, but I was lying to myself. And I feel bad that I drug you into this shit. But I'ma be with Keisha. You can keep the house and I'ma always make sure you and my daughter are good."

"You a bitch ass nigga! How the fuck you leave your wife for some stripper bitch? I—"

"Chill out with all that shit. I'ma come get my shit in the morning—"

"It's already morning, dumb ass. It's fucking three o'clock in the morning. Don't even bother coming to get your shit, because I'ma bleach and burn the shit."

"Bet. Just hit me up if you need anything." I hung up the phone. Everything I had, I worked my ass off for. Clothes, jewelry, and shoes. But none of that shit mattered when it came to Keisha. I'd rock a Walmart outfit and be living in my car rather than go back home to my wife.

"The room is paid up to 2 pm," I heard Keisha say as I opened my eyes. The sun was shining through the curtains, letting me know it was sometime past 6 am. Keisha's ass was fully dressed and she was brushing them little hairs on her forehead.

"You leaving?"

"Yup."

"So what was the point of last night?" I asked, confused.

"Some shit that shouldn't have happened. I love you, Shawnie, but I'm not about to play second to no fucking body."

"I told Dejah the truth. That I want to be—"

"I'm getting married next week," Keisha damn near shouted.

"Damn, how long you been dealing with this nigga?"

"It doesn't matter. It's about time I start doing me. Bernard loves me and—"

"But do you love him?" I got up and got into Keisha's space. "Don't be like me and rush to marry the wrong person because you trying to prove a point that you are over us."

"I'm not you." Keisha pulled away from me. "Go back to your wife. You wasn't wanting me when you was in that bitch's face. Remember I was fucking the opps? I wasn't loyal? But your daughter ain't even born and you trying to do that chick dirty. Why would I want that karma of being with a man who had to leave his pregnant wife first? Yeah, I'm good." Keisha grabbed up her shit and left.

Damn.

I fucked up. I should have been told Keisha how I felt. And now I had lost her forever. I wasn't going back to Dejah. Shit was over. But I didn't even care about that. It was the fact that this fucked up world didn't want me to be with my forever bae.

✺ 10 ✺

JAYSON

I t felt so good to be walking out the Florida Department of Corrections a free man. Last night I was in the Florida State Prison, and today I woke up in the South Florida Reception Center to be processed out. I did twenty years for drug trafficking and killing some low-level drug dealer. I didn't personally shoot him, but I ordered the hit. He worked for Ashton, aka Bando's father. The nigga should have realized he was selling drugs on the wrong side of Miami. The shit started a drug war. Shit was tit for tat. Ashton killed Maya. I ended up killing Ashton. I had killed a lot of people, but the only murder they could prove was the death of a corner boy. And only then because niggas was snitching to the feds for a reduced sentence. But nobody could keep me down, and while it took a minute, I was finally free. I killed my number and now it was time to settle some scores.

"I really appreciate you being here." I grinned as I looked at Tia. Her ass done got finer and it was bittersweet that I didn't do her right in the past. I wanted Kimberly's dad's connections, I lusted Maya, but I loved Tia. I loved my daughter, Jaya, but her mom wasn't my first choice. I was young and stupid putting my hands on Tia because I was so insecure about losing her. Tia had that Tika Sumpter beauty, and so I beat her down so that she wouldn't know her true potential. I wanted her to myself and still lost her. I just hoped that Tia would allow me to right my wrongs.

"I'm only here on the strength of you helping my son. That's it." Tia stood up straight since she was leaning against her car.

"Can I take you to dinner?" I offered. I wanted to spend some time with her.

"No. Where can I drop you off at?" Tia questioned as she drove back toward Miami.

"At my sister's. Damn, it's like that?"

"Yeah, it's like that. Jayson, we ain't good and we never will be." That shit shut me up. I didn't know how to react to that, so it remained quiet between us for the next ten minutes as we got closer to Miami Gardens. The only sound came from the radio.

"T, I was young and dumb." I broke the silence. "And I never really got the chance to say I'm sorry for how bad of a husband I was. I know we can't get the past back. And as fine as you are, I know you got a man. But I at least want to be your friend."

"But you want to kill my brother?" Tia looked at me briefly before giving her attention back to the road.

"He killed my daughter. You can drop the act with me. You didn't want to deal with Ace back then, so why pretend you care now?"

Tia knew her brother was crazy; shit, everybody did. She was fearful of what he would do to her and eventually her kids. So, I wasn't understanding why she was apprehensive of me putting a bullet in his head.

"He's still my brother. You blew the bag. You are the one that had Trinity as your middle man. She don't know shit about this life. Then she gave the drop money to Trap Star. I hate to say it, but that's how she got killed. If you had a more solid team, then you wouldn't have been butt hurt when Isaiah cut you off. You are the one that reached out to Ace about him being your plug after shit went left with Isaiah. I didn't even know my brother was selling drugs let alone know he was hitting all my son's spots. You are the one that brought all this heat. This is your drama."

"And that's exactly why I'm going to handle it. But you still got to make a choice too. I'm not the only one holding secrets, T," I spoke as the car came to a stop at the light off of FL-817 and Ali Baba Avenue. "All I'm saying is that you ain't got to do none of this shit alone. We started this shit together. You can't keep hiding secrets from Isaiah. You see how that shit went for me." I tried to reason with Tia. I lost one daughter and my last living daughter hated me. I done a lot of foul shit, and now I was paying the price for it.

"When the time is right, I'ma tell Isaiah everything. About you. About my brother. But right now isn't the time."

"I wasn't even talking about that. I was saying when are you going to tell—"

"I'd lose everything. I can't just do that to my son."

"Either you tell him or he finds out on his own. And neither one of us wants that."

Pop, Pop

Glass flew every fucking where as shots rang out through the car. There was nowhere to take cover as I tried to duck down in the seat. Tia was trying to shoot back, but there were at least three guns being shot coming from the other vehicle. I was too old for this shit. I tried to kick open my car door and drag me and Tia out, but the door was jammed.

We were stuck. I had to think fast as I shoved Tia to the passenger side of the car and tried to peel off. A train was coming, so I had to turn right and get us the fuck up out of there.

"The fuck was that shit? I know we got enemies, but damn." I tried to slow down my driving so as not to alert the po-pos, and checked the rearview to make sure that we weren't being followed.

"I don't even know," Tia responded. "Niggas must know you home."

"Damn, that was quick. Them little niggas can't even shoot. All them bullets and didn't hit..." I looked over at Tia and she was unresponsive and slumped over.

The blood was seeping through her shirt and I began to panic. "T? Tia? Don't be fucking playing!" I managed to steer the wheel with one arm and tried to shake Tia with the other. I tried to feel for a pulse and didn't feel nothing.

"Tia! Fuck!" I slammed my fist into the steering wheel. Here I was fresh out of prison and the woman that I was trying to make shit right with was dead. I could not ride around with this dead body and even though the city had changed so much, I needed to get my hands on a shovel and a place to bury Tia.

🌣

"Daddy?" Jaya acted like she seen a ghost as she held my grand-baby on her hip when she opened her front door.

"I'm home!" I hugged Jaya and kissed Israel on the forehead. I knew this baby was my granddaughter since she looked just like Jaya when she was little. "Damn, you can't let your dad in?" I looked at Jaya strangely.

I could see the hesitation in her face, but she stepped aside to let me into her home.

"What happened?" Jaya didn't take her eyes off of me.

"I killed my number. No parole. No halfway house. I'm free."

"Oh. But I was talking about the blood on your shirt."

I looked down at the specks of Tia's blood on my shirt. Today had been so hectic that I didn't have time to change my clothes. Shit, even if I had time, there was no way I could walk into any store to buy a shirt. "This shit is old. When you get out of prison they give you your old clothes. I was doing so much twenty years ago, I couldn't even tell you where this came from."

"Oh. So you out, huh?"

"Jay, I know that I been on some bullshit lately, but I'm trying to change that."

"They gave you life. How are you out?" Jaya ignored everything I said.

"Damn, you the police now?" Jaya was worried about the wrong shit. It was none of her business how I was out. "I got paroled—"

"But you just said you off parole." Jaya shifted the baby in her arms.

"I been locked down since you was four years old. I been having to raise you behind bars. When yo' mama died, I did the best I could. Out here trying to provide for you and got caught up. I know I dropped the ball these last few months as a father, but damn, Jay. Your sister dead and you would have thought that family would mean something more to you. How you mad that they let your dad out?"

"I'm not mad. But, Daddy, you know we ain't been talking. You been lying to me and I feel like you still lying to me."

"I'm not lying. But at the same time, everything ain't for you to know."

Jaya didn't need to know everything that was going on. She wasn't my muthafucking mother, I was the parent and it was taking everything in me not to get in her ass for questioning me. I was trying to change and not pop off every time shit didn't go right.

"Can I at least hold my grandbaby?" I reached for Israel and she smiled.

Jaya didn't speak as my granddaughter giggled in my arms. "You know who I am? I'm your pop pop." I bounced Israel and she just grinned.

"Babe, why didn't you wake me up?" I looked over at Ice and he was standing there in some basketball shorts and nothing else. I looked at Ice as a son, but I didn't like him dealing with my daughter. He was too much like me and I didn't want Jaya to be with nothing like me. I wanted her to be with a square nigga not a dope boy. He was a step up from Trap Star's bitch ass. But damn, could Jaya find a nigga that ain't fucked her sister?

It felt like forever as Ice and I stared each other down. Nigga didn't even know I watched his ass come out the pussy. And he had the audacity to stare at me like he wanted to take it there. But my love for Tia made me fall back on going off about him fucking both my daughters. He didn't have to, but he stepped up and took care of Israel and Isaiah Jr. And a nigga couldn't do nothing but respect that.

"How you been?" I tried to cut the tension in the room.

"Good. I'ma get you them—"

"We ain't got to talk business right now. As a matter of fact, don't even worry about that." This was not a place or time to talk shop. As a man, Ice should not be talking about business around Jaya. The less she knew the better. So when the feds came asking questions, she couldn't tell shit because she didn't know shit.

"Bet. Have you talked to my mom?"

"Nah. I'ma try to holla at her later though."

"I tried to call her but she ain't been answering."

"You know what, she did shoot me a text saying she had some shit to handle," I lied.

"Okay. I got to get in these streets. Holla at me." Ice walked toward the bathroom.

Jaya waited to for Ice to turn on the shower before she addressed me. "You been out what? A few hours? How Ms. Tia gonna text you and you ain't got no phone?"

I didn't want to call my daughter out her name, but this bitch was on my hat like she was Sergeant Olivia Benson.

❧ 11 ❧

ICE

"Yo' dad left?" I walked up on Jaya from behind, wrapping my arms around her as she watched Israel sleeping in the crib.

"Yeah. How does he know your mom?" Jaya turned to face me.

"I don't even fucking know," I honestly replied. "But she been working with him about this drug shit."

"I don't trust him, Isaiah."

"I don't either. But a nigga would have been working at McDonald's if he didn't front me that bread."

"How much he give you?"

"You don't even want to know. But I been thinking I don't want to keep doing this shit. I'm making moves to leave this drug shit alone."

"What would you do instead?"

"I haven't even thought that far ahead."

"I get it. I'm barely realizing what I want."

"What, me?"

"I'ma always want you." Jaya wrapped her arms around my neck.

"You better." I gripped Jaya's waist.

"I was thinking, after you handle shit tonight, I'ma see if Keisha or my auntie can watch the baby and we do something. Get out the house."

"I'm with it." I leaned in and kissed Jaya.

I threw on my shoes since I was already dressed and hopped into my whip. I wanted to lay up with my girl and my daughter, but I needed to get to the trap. Even though my mom was MIA, I knew her ass was going to be hitting me up before the night was over about her money.

It was both a blessing and curse that my mom was the plug. She didn't want this life for me. She wanted me to go to college and do better than her. Me getting into selling drugs was not for survival like most niggas. My mom been selling drugs since I could remember, so I wasn't going without. She may have wanted me to be legit, but the lifestyle of the plug was too alluring for me to stay away.

I just didn't see the point of going to college for ten years to be a doctor, going into student loan debt, and only making a few hundred thousand a year. It wasn't appealing. I was thinking about leaving the dope game, but my mom been doing this shit all my life and hadn't so much as gotten a parking ticket. But at the same time, her story was rare. Most of the niggas selling drugs wasn't making it far. I just didn't know what the game plan was when I did leave. How the fuck was I going to take care of my family if all I knew was to flip keys?

I called Carlise about coming to get these bricks for distribution.

"What it do, bro?" I had to laugh to myself that Jaya even believed her father that I was fucking Carlise. Carlise was a straight nigga, rubber dick and all. I forgot half the time that she was a female.

"Not shit. About to pull up to the spot."

"Have you heard from Moms?" Carlise questioned. My mom had taken Carlise under her wing and when it came to this drug shit, I trusted Carlise almost as much as my mom.

SOMEONE TO CALL BAE 3

"I was about to ask you the same thing. You know her ass be doing her own shit."

"You right. Her ass better quit thinking she's grown."

"Facts, bro. I'm about to get in here and get these bricks together. I'll see you in a minute."

"I'ma slide through once I get in traffic."

"Bet." I ended the call with Carlise as I hopped out the car.

It was about to be a long night of getting these keys together, but I couldn't feed my family if I didn't. Jaya's ass could tell herself all she wanted that her ass was independent, but I was paying for real estate school and had gotten my daughter out of them damn Walmart clothes. How the fuck Izzy be in Burberry and Israel wearing some Geranimals shit? If one child was rocking designer then my other one was too. Now if I could get her ass to move back home, I would feel a lot better.

"The fuck?" The words slipped my mouth as Jayson and I made eye contact. All kind of red flags were popping up. One, how the fuck he know about this trap house? Two, how did he get in her?. And lastly, why was there literally blood on his hands?

Jayson's eyes engulfed with darkness, and I was reaching for my gun.

"I don't trust him, Isaiah." Jaya's words echoed in my head. If Jayson's own daughter didn't trust him, then what the fuck did I look like to trust him?

I had my gun trained on Jayson's face as he slowly raised his hands. I didn't see a lick of fear in his eyes as his mouth cracked a smile.

"You really should have been my son, Isaiah."

The nigga was being weird and I couldn't make out what was going on.

"I don't give a fuck how much money I owe you—"

"It's not what you think. But I need you to lower that gun, son. I need to show you something." Jayson's eyes continued to flicker in darkness as he stepped aside to reveal the darkness of the hallway, the only light coming from one of the bedrooms I used to crash in sometimes when I was too tired to go home.

This was starting to feel like some scary movie shit and I was the aloof white girl that was about to get killed. "Nah, you got me fucked up, my nigga!"

And this nigga just got out of prison? I done heard about niggas fucking niggas and not giving a fuck that no means no. Was this the reason he fronted me the money? I was really tired of muthafuckas thinking that because I was light skinned that I was some bitch nigga. I would kill a nigga first before I let them get close to my booty.

"Your mom is back there."

That's all I needed to hear as I bypassed Jayson and went into the closed room. I wasn't emotional, but seeing my mom's body did something to me.

"The fuck happen to her?" I yelled over my shoulder, scared to touch the corpse-like figure in front of me.

"I got shot," my mom grumbled as she flicked open her eyes. I'm not going to lie, my OG was looking bad as she laid there hooked up to all this medical shit. How the hell did Jayson get all this stuff in there?

"I couldn't take her to the hospital. But I know a doctor that do medical on the side. He had to perform surgery and all back here," Jayson spoke as he stood next to me by the bed.

"Ma, what happened. Who shot you?" I was hot. I ain't never seen my mom with so much as a cold, and seeing her like this was not sitting well with me.

"I don't know." My mom's voice croaked. "But I'm going to handle it."

"No the fuck you ain't. You going to concentrate on getting better. Me and Carlise will handle everything," I reassured my mom.

Here I was trying to leave this dope shit alone, and now it was looking like I wasn't leaving any time soon.

12

JAYA

It was the fourth time I had called Ice and his ass was still sending me to voicemail. I had to pay and beg Keisha to watch Israel. My auntie Key was on some hot girl shit and said she wasn't watching no damn kids.

I was dressed too cute in my neon red dress that laced up the sides from top to bottom. It was literally busting at the seams with my fat ass and tig ol' bitties, all thanks to having Israel. I was slim thick. I'd been prepping since Ice left my house. Got my nails done, bought a three-hundred-dollar, free-part wig, and got a Brazilian wax. And now this nigga wasn't answering the phone.

"Girl, this baby is bad as fuck," Keisha commented as soon as I answered the phone.

"Don't be calling my baby bad." I giggled. "What she doing?"

"Crawling around and fucking with shit. I thought you was going out?"

I plopped down on the couch and huffed. "This nigga ain't answering the phone."

"The fuck? See, this is why I only fuck with old niggas now. My man at home right now sleep. Ten o'clock rolls around and this nigga be out for the night."

"I'm good. I ain't fucking with no old nigga." I rolled my eyes. "I'ma take this shit off and come get my baby."

"Don't do that. Go get you a rose."

"Buy myself some flowers? I hate fucking roses."

"No! A pussy sucker rose. I can Cashapp you some money. Go grab you one, come home, and fuck the shit out of yourself."

"I don't even want any dick. I just wanted to spend some quality time with Ice. I know he be in the trap, but damn, he knew I had to beg Keisha's mean ass to watch Israel and I had to pay her," I replied in third person like Keisha wasn't there.

"I am not mean. And bitch, I asked you for two dollars so I can get a blunt wrap. And the way Israel's ass been tearing up my shit, I should have charged you two hundred dollars. I ain't never fucking having kids. This shit is too hard. And her ass shitted on herself. Heffa didn't even say I got to go boo boo or nothing."

"Girl, I hope you changed my baby."

"Yeah, I changed her shitty ass."

Knock, Knock

"Girl, that's Ice now." I quickly put back on my heels. "Here I come!"

"See? Calling me tripping for no reason. Have fun, bitch, and come get your bad ass daughter tomorrow."

"Bye, heffa." I slid my phone to the red to end the call.

"Babe—" I was stopped in my tracks when I saw it was Ace standing on my porch.

"What up, Jay. I think I dropped my watch somewhere in your house."

"Damn. Come in. I'll help you find it." I closed my door behind Ace.

"Where you going all dressed up?" Ace looked me up and down, and I saw the glimmer of lust in his eyes and I wasn't offended by it at all.

"It looks like nowhere." I rolled my eyes as I began to look around my house for Ace's watch. My house wasn't dirty, but that didn't mean that a watch couldn't get lost in my home.

"Where was you supposed to go?"

"My boyfriend was going to take me out, but he ain't answering."

"I don't want you sitting in the house not doing shit. Did you get a babysitter too?"

"Yes!"

"I can always replace the watch. Let me take you out. I know this slam poetry place downtown. And they got some of the best food in the city."

"You don't have to do that. I'ma just order some food and watch a movie."

"Jay, come on. You been working, going to school, and raising your daughter. Let me treat you to a good time." Ace reached his hand out to me with a smile.

"Okay." I rolled my eyes but smiled.

I was a hood chick, but the ambiance of the new Miami Urban Grind coffee shop was lit. Everybody was dressed like they was on their way to Wakanda, and I was dressed like I was on my way to a City Girls concert. I was feeling some type of way as almost everybody's eyes were on me. I saw how a few bitches mugged me, but all the niggas was drooling.

"I want to thank everyone for coming out tonight. Coming to the stage, one of the best to ever do it...Devonta Reese!" the host announced as Ace pulled out my chair at a table toward the front.

"How y'all doing? This poem right here comes from a place of both love and lust." The woman with long, neat locs softly spoke into the mic.

Love being felt caressively, so sexually,
intimately, intensively makes me feel so
radical, speaking hypothetical-ly of how it
makes me feel,
So real, the thrill I always feel, the ideal of me wanting to kiss,
I can't resist what this is, which is you only you.
No one else has made me feel what I felt,

get me so hot until the point I melt,
Our sweat began to pelt upon each other,
There is no other that makes me feel what I
feel when we together for now until forever.
The LOVE we feel physically, mentally and emotionally.
But just to think I'm only speaking hypothetically.

As soon as Davonta finished, the room erupted into finger snapping and encouragement. This was something I had never experienced, but I liked the poem. I thought of Ice and even checked my phone during the poem to see if he called or texted. I even texted Carlise to see if she heard from him, and she told me he was handling some shit. Probably some bitches, because Ice had never left me on read like he was doing now.

"You alright?" Ace watched me as I looked down at my phone for the umpteenth time.

"Yeah." I quickly turned my screen off and made eye contact with Ace.

"Checking to see if your boyfriend strikes you back?"

Damn, I guess I was that obvious. "Yeah. I don't like to be ignored. Like, he was supposed to have come to the house at like six. Here it is ten and he ain't text or call."

"Maybe something happened to him."

"Ain't nothing happen to that nigga." I rolled my eyes. "His sister said she just talked to him." I had enough sense not to elude that Isaiah was a drug dealer. As much as I was mad at him, I wasn't about to be dry snitching to no fucking body.

"You hungry?" Ace changed the subject because there was nothing to say about how Ice had stood me up. "You should try the red beans and rice or shrimp and grits."

"I haven't met nobody yet that can fuck with me when it comes to some red beans and rice."

"Oh, you be cooking like that?"

"I told you I help my cousin with his food truck. Hell, I taught him how to cook."

"You take care of your daughter, beautiful, can cook, working, and going to school. And this nigga acting up?"

"I'm saying!" I co-signed on Ace gassing me up. "He better quit playing with me."

"For somebody else snatch you up." Ace stared at me with intent, and I had to fight the urge to lean in and kiss his thick lips.

"Right." I quickly averted my eyes to the menu in front of me. "I think I'ma do the shrimp and grits." I tried to concentrate on anything but Ace's fine ass.

"You going to like it. You from Miami?"

"Born and raised. You?"

"The Dominican Republic."

"Really? My cousin is Haitian on his dad's side, so we would go to Haiti every summer." I perked up since both Haiti and the DR were a part of the island Hispaniola.

"Damn. That's what's up. So, you speak Spanish and Creole? Or just Creole?"

"Just Creole. Not a lot though. You speak Spanish?"

"Fluently."

"So does my boyfriend." I tried to remind both me and Ace that I had a man.

"He's from Miami too?"

"Yeah. But his family is from Cuba."

"That's what's up," Ace replied as the waitress sat our food in front of us.

Ace was right about the food, and for the next few minutes it was silence as we ate. I was full, but I wasn't ready to go home. And yet Ice still hadn't called or texted me. This was some straight bullshit. There wasn't enough trapping in the world for him to not answer the phone. I was mad and ready to go home.

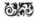

What the fuck was I doing?

You would have thought that I didn't get no dick the way I let Ace touch me. I had let Ace convince me to come to his house, and I wasn't here a whole ten minutes before I was letting Ace rub his hands down my body. I ain't going to lie, the shit felt so good.

It didn't help that I had a couple drinks at the poetry slam and now they had hit me because I was buzzed.

"You know I got a man?" I commented before Ace's and my lips connected.

"And? Ain't the nigga been ignoring you all night?" Ace leaned me back on his couch and my dumb ass let him.

Ace found himself in between my legs, and I could feel his dick from his jeans against my thigh, and his ass was packing. My panties were soaking wet from the anticipation of new dick. I was by far not a hoe, but at this moment, I was on some bald-headed hoe shit.

"Let's say I'd been trying to get into this good ass HBCU college for years. I thought I would never get in. So, I settled to go to a community college. Finally, the HBCU has an opening. Why would I stay at the community college when I have the chance at my dream?" Ice's words took up all the space in my mind and guilt washed over me.

What the fuck was I doing?

"Can you take me to Keisha's?" I pushed Ace back.

"What's wrong?"

"This shit ain't right. I got a good man and I'm over here doing this shit." I sat up. I wanted to fuck Ace, and if I didn't have a boyfriend, I would. But I didn't have it in me to cheat on Isaiah.

"You really trying to be faithful to the nigga that been ignoring you all night? You are too beautiful to be putting up with a man that plays games."

I couldn't let Ace cloud my judgement on my man. I looked back at all the years that Ice been down with me. He took on a baby that didn't belong to him, and even though I wanted to live on my own, Ice made sure me and Israel didn't go without. Ice was a dope boy and he was out there risking his life for me and Israel. And what was I doing? Spread eagle on a couch with a nigga I had no business being with. I felt lower than low.

"Can you take me to Keisha's? Or I can just get a Uber." I stood to pull down my dress. I didn't want to let Ace put doubt in my mind when he wanted to fuck me. If anybody knew Isaiah, it was me. He wasn't a cheater. And the only one that was fucking up was me. I couldn't believe I had let shit get this far.

"My bad. Look, I'm attracted to you, and I know you're attracted to me. But I don't want you feeling bad about it. And more than anything, I don't want to lose you as a friend." Ace stood up and towered over me. He and Ice were like night and day. Light skin and dark skin. Ice was more of a thug, while Ace was more laid back. Ace, from what I saw, was a good man, but he wasn't my man.

"Me either." I smiled all fake. I didn't trust myself to continue being friends with Ace. Because I knew me, and there was no way I was going to stay faithful with Ace's fine ass waiting on the side for Ice to fuck up. Yeah, that wasn't about to go down. And as much as I appreciated him helping me prepare for my real estate license, I had to cut his ass off.

"Bitch, don't come waking this baby up." Keisha swung her front door open after Ace dropped me off.

I gave Keisha my middle finger as I crossed the threshold. But Keisha was right, if Israel got up, her ass was going to be up all night wanting to play.

"Where's Ice?" Keisha grabbed a sack of zaza off the coffee table and began to roll up.

"I don't know." I sat down on the couch across from Keisha.

"Huh?"

"I didn't go out with Ice. I went with Ace."

"Girl! What the fuck you mean you went out with Ace?"

"Ice left me on read. I don't know what's going on. Ace popped up at my house and took me out. The next thing I know, I'm under him on his couch."

"Bitch, you don't have to smash everybody that you like."

"You got some nerve. Your body count is at what, seventy-five? Mine is still two. And why you talking, we didn't fuck."

"You tried it. My body count is only one more than you. I knew this was going to happen. Now I feel bad."

"Why do you feel bad? You didn't do nothing."

"I thought I was helping by putting you in touch with someone who could help you get a place. I knew the nigga was fine. A blind bitch could see he was fine. Now look at this shit."

"It's not your fault. It's mine. I knew what the fuck I was doing when I agreed to go to his house, and it wasn't for no damn bible study. I'm just relived that I didn't fuck him. Because, baby? Nigga working with at least eight inches. It literally took the power of the Lord for me not to fuck him."

"You better than me. Because I ended up fucking Shawnie and I'm getting married in four days."

I giggled, because I already knew. Shawnie called me that day because he needed to come stay with me since he had left Dejah. He was living between me, Ice, and Auntie Key until he got his own place. His ass refused to go back home. "I know. Why you do my cousin like that?"

"He is married, Jaya."

"You wasn't worried about that when you was letting him knock you down. You know you love that nigga. Bitch, we been best friends since we was six. And I know for a fact that you been in love with him since day one. Don't marry Mr. Otis. You going to regret it."

"Why does everybody keep saying that?"

"Because it's the truth."

"I just can't accept the fact that he didn't choose me first."

"He did, Kesh. You was with Tommy. Y'all's shit is complicated."

"I am getting married. Bernard really loves me. He's safe."

"He's old enough to be your daddy. You do what you want. But do what makes you happy."

"I know. At the end of the day, I got to do what is best for Keisha. My period was supposed to start yesterday. And if I'm pregnant, I don't know who the daddy is."

"Bitch, what the fuck?"

"Girl, why am I always involved in some bullshit?"

"Me too. My shit is worse. Me and my dead sister got the same baby daddy. Girl, I will take a free trip to Maury any day over my daughter and nephew being brother and sister," I replied as I took the blunt from Keisha. "Now this nigga want to call."

"Who?"

"Isaiah's punk ass." I slid my phone to answer. Even though I chose Isaiah, I still was mad that his ass had been ignoring me all day. "What, nigga?"

"My bad, babe. My mom got shot."

All my anger dissolved and was replaced with guilt. My future mother-in-law had gotten shot, and my nasty ass was hugged up with a nigga. "Is she okay? What hospital y'all at?"

"It's kind of touch and go right now. But she conscious. We at the trap."

"What?"

"Long story. Remember how I told you I was fighting with this nigga?"

"Yeah."

"I think it was one of his people. I don't know for sure. Maybe even one of Gio's people. You at home? Where's my daughter? "

"No, we at Keisha's."

"Okay. Just stay there. Let me get some shit situated and I'ma come get y'all. Love you."

I felt so bad for my actions tonight. That's what my problem was, jumping to conclusions, and now this shit just might cost me my relationship.

❧ 13 ❧

TIA

"**I** need to talk to you." I tried to sit up, but my wounds said otherwise. I was trying to stay optimistic, but I didn't know if I was going to make it to tomorrow or not. And as far as I was concerned, I couldn't go to the grave with all these secrets.

"Ma, you alright?" Isaiah's eyes filled with worry and concern.

"Yeah, I'm alright. I got some shit to tell you. Jayson is my ex-husband."

"What?"

"We met in Cuba when I was fifteen and—"

"Is he my dad?"

"No. But you were supposed to be his son."

"Ma, come on now. We don't do secrets. Why would you not tell me knowing I'm fucking his daughter?"

"I didn't know that Jaya was his daughter until recently. I didn't want—"

Isaiah cut me off again. "Ma, we can't be moving like this. I don't trust nobody in this world like I trust you. So when you came to me and said that you would handle shit with Jayson, I fell back because you my OG and your word is bond."

"I know. Me and Jayson had a shaky past." I didn't want my

burdens to be my son's, and I opted out of telling him the truth about how Jayson used to fuck my ass up. "If it wasn't for him today, I would not be alive. I couldn't go to the hospital. I lay in the back of a van until they could set up this makeshift hospital room. It looks bad, but it's not. The two bullets grazed me. I passed out from shock. Basically, a really bad rug burn. I don't want this beef with you and him to keep going. I want you to live your life. I'm not saying that Jayson didn't do some wrong shit, but I'm not so innocent either." I laid out my feelings.

If anybody would have asked me how I felt about Jason yesterday or either this morning, I would have said fuck that nigga. But he saved my life. He could have buried me and kept it moving, but instead, he found a doctor, and it was my idea to use one of the traps."

I wasn't really no different from Jayson, I hid shit from my kids too. I was knocking Jayson for having Trinity help him, but I was my son's plug. I didn't want this life for him. He chose this shit, and I be damned if I left him out here to figure out this drug game on his own.

I had held a grudge about Jayson for so long, and now it was time to let it go. When it came to Jayson, from now on, I would pick peace. I hoped he could do the same with my brother.

"I don't know what you want me to say, Ma. I mean, this nigga was trying to break-up me and Jaya. She don't trust him. I don't trust him."

"I know," I huffed. "He didn't want shit to get this bad between all of us. I'm not justifying what he did, but I understand it."

"Bet." I could see that Isaiah was upset. And if he was this upset about Jayson, he wasn't going to be able to handle the truth of feuding with his uncle.

"Isaiah—"

"I got to go get Jaya and the baby."

"Don't be mad at me, son."

"I'm not even mad." Ice stood up and left.

"That didn't go well at all." Jayson came into the room.

"Not at all. I don't want me and my son at odds with each other. He got to know that I did all this to protect him," I spoke as Jayson kissed my forehead. "You about to leave?"

"Hell nah. Tia, I meant what I said when I said that I've changed. Too many people have died for me to be on that toxic Ike Turner shit."

"I saw who shot me," I blurted out. If I didn't see the shit happen my damn self, I wouldn't have believed it. If this didn't teach me nothing else, it taught me that no one could be trusted.

❧ 14 ❧

KEISHA

"Y ou nervous?" Bernard asked me as we pulled up to his
sister's house.

I swallowed hard and replied, "Yes."

I met most of Bernard's family at Sidney's wedding and they
seemed nice. But now that I was marrying Bernard, I didn't
know how they would react to me. I was twenty-three and he
was forty-eight. I was only a few years older than his daughter.
Hell he was old enough to be my daddy.

I was hood, loud, outspoken, and gave zero fucks about who
liked me or not. I was a bougie stripper that had her own bag.
And here was Bernard who was suburban, meek, and wanted
everyone to get along. He went out of his way to make sure I was
happy and loved. We met at WAWA and he fell in love from day
one. If I was in my forties, I could see myself with Bernard, but I
was too wild to be tied down to him or anybody else. If I had to
pick between Bernard and Shawnie, I would pick Shawnie, but I
wasn't about to entertain no married man. So, I was going with
Bernard.

"My family loves you."

"So they okay with you being with a stripper half your age?
Because I know if I was them, I wouldn't be."

"They understand that everyone's life is different. And they respect that sex work is a means for income."

"Sex work? Why it sounds like you saying I'm selling pussy."

"Sorry, love. Adult entertainment."

I didn't know why, but the way Bernard described me, I felt a little dirty. "Umm...yeah."

"They already like you." Bernard smiled as he held my hand and killed the engine.

Bernard led me inside the home and it seemed like everyone stopped what they were doing. Bernard had a huge family. He had three brothers, two sisters, parents, one daughter, and bunch of nieces, nephews, and cousins. I had zero family outside of Shawnie's small family. My mom was an only child and so was my grandma. So when they died, I had no natural family members.

"Keisha!" Bernard's sister Vanessa wrapped her arms around me in a hug. "How you been? Tanya, come meet Bernard's fiancée." Vanessa ushered me around to both familiar and unfamiliar faces.

"Wow, you're so beautiful."

"Congratulations on the wedding."

"How are you, Keisha?"

Bernard's family surrounded me with positive vibes. I had never felt this type of love in abundance. And I ain't going to lie, it felt good to be wanted. I didn't know why they liked me so much. They all had careers and graduated from HBCUs. Everyone was friendly and I felt at home.

"Hey, stepmom!" Sidney walked into the house and hugged me.

It felt weird to hang out with Sidney since she was my age and was going to become my stepdaughter. I was hood and I didn't know shit about being a mother let alone being a stepmother.

"Where's your husband?" I asked Sidney.

"He has lectures all day."

I didn't know what her ass was talking about, so I just grinned.

"Keisha, would you like a beer? We got IPAs, a few Belgium lagers, Porter, and some blonde Ale," Vanessa asked me as she walked over to me.

"You got some regular beer?" I questioned. Then I thought about my possible pregnancy. "You know what? I'll just have some water."

"I got you, girly." Vanessa walked off.

"See, I told you, you had nothing to worry about. My family loves you." Bernard walked up on me.

Being around Bernard's family made my decision even easier. I was going to be with Bernard, and Shawnie needed to work out shit with his wife.

※

"You look so pretty!" Jaya grinned as she watched me spin around in my wedding dress.

"I'm getting married, girl!" I shouted as I admired the beauty of my wedding gown.

"You are. I'm so happy for you, best friend."

"You think I'm making the right choice?" I turned to face Jaya. My nerves were all over the place. I didn't know if I could let myself move on from Shawnie.

"No," Jaya flat out said.

"What should I do?"

"Leave."

"What about Bernard?"

"Tell him the truth. That you don't—"

"I think I'm going to be sick." I rushed off to the adjoining bathroom of the hotel suite.

Bernard had gone all out to make this day special for us. The theme wasn't really my taste, but it had that classy feel. I wasn't feeling the music choices either, all old people music, but I appreciated Bernard for making this day so special.

I hadn't had anything to eat, but I was feeling queasy as I emptied clear bile into the toilet. Jaya was real life my best friend, and she moved my hair out the way and rubbed my back as I continued to vomit.

I was sick to my stomach as I rinsed my mouth out with some hotel mouthwash. I damn near crawled to the bed. As I closed my eyes, I felt like I'd upchucked my whole stomach.

"Kesh, you need to take a pregnancy test."

"I'm not pregnant."

"You don't know that."

"Right now isn't the right time for me to be having no baby. Shit, I don't want no damn kids. Bitch, you see this body? How the hell am I going to be twerking up and down the pole and I got a beer gut?"

"I don't have no beer gut." Jaya got defensive.

"No, but you got all them stretch marks. I can't do crying, the diapers, all that moving. Hell to the nah. Not everybody is meant to be a mother, and I'm one of them."

"You say that now, but I think you would be a good mom."

"How and I don't know who the daddy is?"

"Chile...that's what Maury is for."

Me and Jaya began to laugh.

"I'm going to marry Bernard. My baby needs stability."

Jaya just looked at me like I had two heads. "I guess."

I'll give you the sun, the rain, the moon, the stars and the mountains
I'll give you the world and all that you wish for
And even more
Girl I'll love you more than you could know
And that's for sure
I'd climb the highest hill, cross the widest sea
Nothing could discourage me
And I pray that you'll be always there for me forevermore, oh
Ready or not

I'll give you everything and more
All that I've got is yours
I'll give you everything
All that you're looking for

No this nigga didn't pick this old ass shit, I thought to myself. Bernard was paying for the wedding and he didn't even consider what I wanted. But what bothered me the most about it, was that I didn't even care. I thought I was going to be nervous when I walked down the aisle, but I was numb. I just wanted to get this shit over with.

Regardless of my doubts, the hotel ballroom was decorated so beautifully. It did have that old lady look, but it was glamorous old lady. Bernard and his family didn't spare any expense.

Bernard looked so sexy standing at the end of the aisle in his black tux. I wasn't usually a fan of light-skinned niggas, but Bernard had that zaddy vibe. He wasn't the finest man, but he was certainly was cute and he loved me.

"Please be seated... Thank you." The pastor addressed the people in attendance. I didn't have any family, so Bernard's family sat on both sides of the aisle.

"Welcome friends, family, and loved ones! We are here today to celebrate as we watch Bernard and Keisha join hands in marriage. We're here to laugh with them, some of you are here to cry. You may have already started, but most of all, we're here to wish them well as they begin their new life together. I'd like to say, on behalf of Keisha and Bernard, thank you all so very much for being here. I know it means a lot to them." The pastor looked at both of us. "To start our ceremony off today, I've asked Keisha and Bernard to write their own vows. Bernard, please proceed."

"Keisha, I knew from the very moment I laid eyes on you that you were my forever. Someway, somehow, I was determined to make you mine. And from this day forward, my heart is entirely yours...."

"As we continue to grow in our lives together, I promise to

give you all of my words when needed, and to share in the silence when they are not, to pick you up if you are down, to love you unconditionally, to lay my bare skin on you when needed most, to care for you and our families for as long as we live, to adventure with you always, to say I love you before falling asleep each night, to be the best man I can be as we grow a family together, and to always know in the deepest part of my soul, that when challenges arise we will always find our way back to one another."

"Ladies and gentlemen, that's what we're here to witness, the entangled roots of these two individuals that are about to join together as one united tree, reaching for the stars together, sharing the same nutrients, weathering the same storms, growing together year after year—some rings thick and healthy, some rings thinner—reminders of the years where things didn't go as planned, or the years that fires hit the reset button all around them.

"Because real love is sharing a life together. Like the poet said, any fool can fall in love. Real love is what comes next. After the fall is over. What happens when you've landed and all around you is normalcy once again and it's time to do the dishes, or pay the bills, or pick up the kids from school.

"There's a great line from another poem by Adrienne Rich that says 'No dust on the furniture of love.' In that poem, the speaker is being tongue in cheek about the difference between falling in love, and the crash landing that happens for so many of us.

"Bernard and Keisha, we all stand here with you today and hold you up in happiness, but in a couple of weeks, maybe a couple of months, maybe even in a couple of years, real life is going to have to creep back in. You will need each other to face those challenges. You will need each other as partners. As equals, fiercely honest with one another and fiercely committed to one another. You have to be both. Honest and committed, because real love demands both, and a successful marriage demands a foundation of real love," the pastor stated.

You have taught me that two people joined together with respect, trust, and open communication can be far stronger and happier than each could ever be alone. You are the strength I didn't know I needed, and the joy that I didn't know I lacked. Today, I choose to spend the rest of my life with you.

    "I promise to encourage your compassion,
    Because that is what makes you unique and wonderful.
    I promise to nurture your dreams,
    Because through them your soul shines.
    I promise to help shoulder our challenges,
    For there is nothing we cannot face if we stand together.
    I promise to be your partner in all things,
    Not possessing you, but working with you as a part of the whole.
    Lastly, I promise to you perfect love and perfect trust,
    For one lifetime with you could never be enough.
    This is my sacred vow to you, my equal in all things."

"Thank you, Bernard." The pastor thanked Bernard for his vows. "Keisha."

Keisha

I, Keisha, take you, Bernard, to be my husband, secure in the knowledge that you will be my constant friend, my faithful partner in life, and my one true love.

On this special day, I give you in the presence of God and all those in attendance, my sacred promise to stay by your side as your faithful *wife*, in sickness and in health, in joy and in sorrow, through the good times and the bad.

I promise to love you without reservation, comfort you in times of distress, encourage you to achieve all of your goals, laugh with you and cry with you, grow with you in mind and spirit, always be open and honest with you, and cherish you for as long as we both shall live.

"Bernard, please repeat after me. Keisha, I give you this ring as a symbol of my promise to love you forever. With it, I promise that I will honor you, cherish you, and love you the rest of my days, regardless of what challenges or triumphs we face together."

"Keisha, I give you this ring as a symbol of my promise to love you forever. With it, I promise that I will honor you, cherish you, and love you the rest of my days, regardless of what challenges or triumphs we face together." Bernard stared into my eyes.

"Keisha, please repeat after me. Bernard, I give you this ring as a symbol of my promise to love you forever. With it, I promise that I will honor you, cherish you, and love you the rest of my days, regardless of what challenges or triumphs we face together."

"Bernard, I give you this ring as a symbol of my promise to love you forever. With it, I promise that I will honor you, cherish you, and love you the rest of my days, regardless of what challenges or triumphs we face together." This was it. I was about to become Mrs. Bernard Rhodes. My emotions were all over the place and there was no turning back.

"Bernard, Keisha, having proclaimed love and commitment to one another in the sight of these witnesses and myself, I am so happy to pronounce you, by the power vested in me by the Greater Bethel African Methodist Episcopal Church and the state of Florida, husband and wife! Bernard, you may kiss your bride!"

Bernard slowly raised my veil and I tried to smile, even though this was supposed to be a happy moment.

"Keisha, if you kiss that nigga, I'ma fuck you and that nigga up!" Everybody turned to see Shawnie coming down the aisle.

Was it wrong that I was smiling?

"This here ain't what you want, youngblood." Bernard stepped forward like he was about to do something. Shawnie had at least a foot on Bernard in height, was at least forty pounds heavier, and half his age. Bernard might have been able to toss niggas back in the nineties, but it was 2021 and I had yet to meet a nigga that could whoop Shawnie's ass.

"I wouldn't do that." I stopped Bernard from taking another step. I was trying to save him from getting his ass whooped in front of his friends and family. Bernard wasn't trying to listen to me, and instead of listening to my warning, he bypassed me.

I just blew out a breath of frustration because Shawnie was about to beat Bernard's ass.

"You're not going to stop him?" Jaya got in my space and whispered loudly. "Shawnie gonna fuck his ass up."

"I tried." I shrugged my shoulders. At this point, there was nothing I could do. And I for damn sure wasn't about to get in between two men as they threw blows.

Before anyone could really react, Shawnie's fist was colliding against Bernard's face. Bernard didn't have a chance as he went flying to the floor. The nigga was sleep before he hit the floor.

"Come on, babe." Shawnie offered his hand as Bernard lay at our feet.

I looked down at a sleeping Bernard and then at Shawnie. In a split second, I had to make a choice. Go with the married man that had my heart or the man that I knew for a fact would make sure I was good? I stepped over Bernard as Shawnie grabbed me up and kissed me. It was so much force behind Shawnie's kiss that I was feeling faint.

"Wait for me!" Jaya ran behind us.

I tried not to make eye contact with anybody. Even though I was openly picking Shawnie, it didn't mean I didn't feel bad about how things played out with Bernard. I was realizing that a life of misery didn't equate to security. I was forcing myself to be with Bernard just so I could have the stability of what he could offer. I really was going to marry him, but Shawnie had rescued me from a life of stable misery.

"I couldn't lose you." Shawnie led me and Jaya to his car.

"What about Dejah?" I needed to know if Shawnie wanted only me or just something for the side.

"I told her when we was at the hotel that it was over. I haven't been back since either. Kesh, there is no other woman I want but you. I'm sorry that I played games. I'm sorry for hurting you. But I don't want to keep hiding how I feel. And nothing or no one is gonna stop me from making shit work between us."

"I'm too old for games, JaShawn." I didn't know what to make of these recent events. I was a real life a runaway bride, and I didn't know what the hell I was going to do with Shawnie's married ass.

"I am too. You really think I would crash your wedding just to be on some fuck boy shit? I'm not on that shit. I'm not asking for you to marry me tomorrow, but I want us to try to make it work."

"While you're married." I stopped in my tracks and folded my arms. "And you about to have a baby." The whole situation had me mad. I was supposed to be Shawnie's first and only wife. I was supposed to be the mother of all his children. We weren't supposed to have outside baby daddies or baby mamas. And now that I might be pregnant, it was looking like both our first kids were going to be by other people. I really wanted Shawnie to be the father, but there was a fifty percent chance that Bernard was the father.

"I don't give a fuck about none of that. I'ma be a father to my daughter, but as far as continuing to be with Dejah, that shit is over."

"I think I'm pregnant." I shared my truth. So much had happened between me and Shawnie that I didn't want to hide nothing else from him.

I waited for Shawnie to react as he stared at me. It seemed like Shawnie wasn't too happy about having two babies on the way. Damn, I was looking like I was trying to trap him, which was far from the truth.

🌿 15 🌿

SHAWNIE

"I love you, JaShawn." Dejah looked up into my eyes. "This is how you want play it?"

"I really didn't set out to hurt you. I thought this was what I wanted. But you can't help who you love."

"So that's why you bring these divorce papers to me?"

I wasn't a cold-hearted nigga. I didn't want to break Dejah's heart, but I couldn't keep up this lie of shit being good. Regardless of my feelings, I'd make sure that Dejah and my daughter were always good. "I want you to be happy. I know—"

"So I guess all them months I held you down in prison didn't mean shit? You pursued me! *Dejah, I love you. Dejah, marry me.* And then we break up. Did you go back to your ex then? Hell fucking no. You at my job. *Dejah, I can't be without you.* What you say? There ain't no breaking up. I been faithful. I drove you around when you got out, I been your freak in the sheets. Fucking you in the car. All that shit. My mom asked me what I was going to do when you went back to your ex. I told her that would never happen. You couldn't just dump me then. Noooo. You wait to marry me and get me pregnant. You wait till I'm emotional and insecure to tell me that everything you said to me was a fucking lie."

"But at the time, that's how I felt. I'ma forever have you and my daughter."

"You think I want that bitch around my daughter? You think I'ma let you play house with my baby? You got me fucked up!"

I wanted to correct Dejah about calling Keisha out her name, but I didn't want to add salt to the wound. "No one can replace you as our daughter's mother. I wouldn't let that shit happen."

"Just like you allowed some hoe to ruin your marriage?"

There wasn't no point in going back and forth. "You hungry? You need anything?" I tried to soften the blow of wanting a divorce.

"I don't want shit from you!" Dejah got hostile.

I didn't want to be an asshole, but that was just me. "Ok. But can you sign the papers?" I wondered. Shit was over, let's make it official.

"Get the fuck out my house!" Dejah shouted as she threw the divorce papers at my head. "You don't give a fuck about me or this baby."

"You want me to come back later to get them or...?" Now why did I say that shit? Dejah began to hit me in my chest and my face. Pregnant or not, I hemmed her up to prevent her from hitting me.

"Let me go!" Dejah fought for me to release her, and so I did. A nigga felt bad as I saw the tears streaming down her face. But my decision was best for everybody involved. I could admit that I was in the wrong for playing games with Dejah. I never set out to hurt her. I really thought I wanted this shit. I convinced myself that I was over Keisha, but me crashing her wedding to Mr. Clarence proved otherwise.

"I can't say this enough. I'm sorry. Ain't no one to blame but me. I thought that—"

"I don't want to hear that shit. A bunch of excuses of why you are leaving your pregnant wife to be with a stripper? Yeah, nigga, I'm good. Get the fuck out!"

There was nothing else to say. From the outside looking in,

Dejah was right. I left my pregnant wife for a stripper. But it was more to it than that. No matter what, Keisha was my forever bitch.

🔯

"Baby, bring me a beer." Me and my cousin both looked from Tia to my uncle.

"Baby?" Jaya repeated out loud.

"What the fuck is going on? Your dad fucking Ms. Tia? When did that shit happen?" I asked Jaya.

"She got shot. Now they in love. He only been out a couple of weeks and now they a couple."

"Zo. The fuck. You, Uncle Jayson, and Ice need to venture out. Because, damn. How the fuck your daughter's adoptive brother is also your dead sister's real baby daddy. And now you fucking your stepbrother. None of y'all think this shit is weird?" I wondered.

"Is it weird that you left your pregnant wife and now you are sleeping in my stepbrother's adoptive daughter's room?" Jaya clapped back.

"Chill out, bro." I waved Jaya off. I was working to get my new place in a few days. Jaya quickly forgot where she came from. Like her ass wasn't sleeping at my house when she first came back to Miami.

"Don't be trying to come for me. Your uncle is the reason for all this drama," Jaya responded as we sat poolside at Ms. Tia's house. It was a surprise to all of us that Uncle Jayson was over here being the Miami "Melvin" of *Baby Boy*. Ms. Tia had invited us to her house for a barbecue. But nobody could expect that Uncle Jayson was here let alone playing house with Ms. Tia. To be honest, the shit was weird. I was just glad it wasn't my problem.

Instead of responding to Jaya, I got up and looked for Keisha. These past two weeks since I crashed Keisha's wedding had been nothing but lit. I was only a few days away from renting me a house. A nigga was low-key homeless, but that didn't stop shit between me and Kesh. I may have been staying with my cousin, but I wasn't no broke, begging, unemployed nigga.

I wasn't the biggest fan of Keisha stripping, but my ass was at King of Diamonds making it rain at least a few nights a week. All them niggas could look at her banging body as she slid down the pole, but I was the only one whose dick she was sliding down. Keisha told me how Tommy was insecure about her dancing, but my baby was out here getting the bag. And I wasn't mad about that shit.

Tia's backyard was huge but not that huge to the point that I couldn't see who was here. So far it was Ms. Tia, Uncle Jayson, Jaya, Isis, and Indica. Ice was on his way. I got up from the lounge chair of the cabana and went into the pool house that was attached to the covered cabana. Even when I was selling drugs, I didn't have nothing as nice as Ms. Tia's house. She real life lived in luxury. The landscape of the backyard alone was three hundred racks. I was working on having some real nice shit. And because I was doing it the legal way, it was taking me a little longer.

And I was cool with that. I didn't ever want to see a prison again. I didn't knock Ms. Tia or Ice's hustle. I just didn't want to give up my freedom. I don't know, but there was something about police pulling up to your place of business or home and them muthafuckas couldn't do shit. Miami Hustle brought all kinds of people out, including twelve. And them niggas always came on some food shit and never about my past or questioning my business. And regardless of me leaving Dejah, I wanted to be present in my daughter's life. I fo' sho' didn't want to be raising her behind bars like my uncle Jayson did Jaya.

"Kesh?" I called out as I stepped inside the pool house.

"I'm in the bathroom!" Keisha responded.

"You good?" I questioned as I walked into the bathroom and saw that Keisha was wiping her mouth and flushing the toilet.

"Damn, how much did you have to drink?" Ms. Tia had the liquor flowing like water, and I knew I already had three shots of Henny, a beer, and some fruity ass cocktail. I was faded.

"I didn't drink no liquor." Keisha made eye contact with me.

"Did you find out if you are pregnant?" I questioned since the shit just popped in my head.

"I didn't want to say nothing yet...but yeah." Keisha diverted her eyes.

"Is it mine?" Keisha had no idea that I was rocking with her if the baby she was carrying was mine or not. I loved every part of her.

"I don't know who the father is."

"How many we talking?"

I knew that Keisha wasn't a hoe, but I also needed clarity that she wasn't fucking with no other nigga.

"Don't even play me like that, JaShawn. It's just you and Bernard. And to be honest, I'm not sure if I want to even keep it."

"Don't do that, Kesh."

"Why do you even care? You about to be a daddy without me." I could hear the pain in her voice. We always talked about having kids and that was the plan when I got out of prison. I never thought to have kids with anyone but her. But I fucked up. And if I could have it that Keisha was the mother of my first-born, then I would do anything for that to happen. But that wasn't the case.

"Babe, I'm sorry. You don't think that shit hurts me too? I love my daughter but I love you and this baby too. I'm not trying to fuck up what we have. Real talk. I'm not going to pressure you to keep the baby. But no matter what, I got you. Ain't shit changed." I brought Keisha into a hug and we stood there, silent.

My mind was racing with all kinds of thoughts. Just that fast, I became the typical hood nigga. It was looking like I had two women pregnant at the same time. I didn't want two baby mamas. I wanted a wife that I loved and she was the only one that had my seeds. But because I let anger and my dick rule my dating life, shit was all the way fucked up. I would never admit it to my kids, but I was happy about Keisha being pregnant. And I wish that I had never met Dejah. Was it fucked up that I already had a favorite child and neither of my kids were here yet?

16

JAYA

"*How the fuck your daughter's adoptive brother is also your dead sister's real baby daddy. And now you fucking your step-brother. None of y'all think this shit is weird?*" Shawnie's words floated around in my head.

It was already bad enough I was in a love triangle with Trinity and Ice. And now my dad was dating my man's mom. I couldn't think of anything more trifling. If there was another secret connection between me and Ice, I was shooting every fucking body. Because this shit made no damn sense. There were over six million people in Miami and I was fucking my sister's man/step-brother. At this point, I had to accept the situation for what it was.

My auntie had Israel, and this pool barbeque was what I needed. There was a cool breeze as I closed my eyes and cleared my mind.

"Hey, sexy." Ice kissed me. "Where everybody at?"

I opened my eyes. "Keisha and Shawnie in the pool house. The twins are in the garage. And my dad and your mom are..." I couldn't bring myself to say what I expected out loud.

"Damn, babe. That's all bad."

"Are you sure you ain't my brother?" I stared at Ice and I was being dead ass serious.

"It's obvious I'm mixed. Where is this coming from?"

"It just seems like no matter who got a secret it affects us. Shawnie is able to cheat on his wife in peace, but my black ass leave my cheating husband and fall in love with my sister's man. And now our parents are trying to rekindle some shit. Did you know that they used to be married?"

"Yeah. I found out the night my mom got shot. I'm not happy about them being together. The shit is weird. But as much as I hate to admit it, if it wasn't for your dad, my mom would have been dead. Do you know how much it costs for all that medical equipment and for your dad to pay a doctor to come to a trap house to operate?"

"Your mom paid for that shit." I rolled my eyes.

"No she didn't. That was all your dad. I know this shit is weird, but just like we got through that shit with Trinity, we're going to get through this."

"I'm not about to be fucking my stepbrother." And my ass was dead ass serious.

"You been fucking your stepbrother." Ice pulled me into him.

"You're fucking nasty!" I giggled as Ice kissed on me.

"Listen, I was mad about them being together, but they're grown. And shit was fucked up between me and my dad. But the nigga broke bread when my back was against the wall. And he saved my mom. So, shit, I ain't got no more animosity toward Jayson. We been through too much for us to be holding grudges."

I side eyed Ice as he spoke.

"Alright. Don't get too happy, but I want us to continue to live separate but I want my engagement ring back."

"Wow."

"What?"

"Where is this coming from?"

I thought about coming so close to fucking another nigga on

SOMEONE TO CALL BAE 3

some jumping to conclusions bullshit. The whole situation had me wanting to not take Isaiah for granted. "I know you trying and I only want to be with you. I got something to tell you though. I—"

"I know you didn't invite this nigga to my mama's house." Isaiah got mad, and I looked around to see Ace as he emerged from coming through the side gate of the backyard.

"I didn't invite him." I watched Isaiah shoot to his feet. My heart was about to beat out of my chest. I wanted to tell Isaiah that I almost cheated, but I didn't want Ace coming to my man's mama's house on some bullshit. I'd been avoiding Ace like the plague and his ass been calling, texting, and popping up at my house. I could only imagine if I gave him some pussy how he would react. The last time I saw Ace, I told him that I wanted to be only platonic friends. The nigga said he respected my decision, but now he was popping up at Ms. Tia's house.

"Nigga, you got to go," Isaiah yelled as he walked over to Ace to confront him. I almost fell in the pool as I tried to catch up with Isaiah.

"Where's Tia?" Ace questioned.

Lord, please don't let this man be messing with Ms. Tia. Didn't he say she reminded him of his sister? I swear this nigga would do anything to get close to me. I didn't know why God cursed me with these good looks and bomb pussy.

"Bando?" I heard my dad speak from behind me. Why did that name sound familiar. "Tia, get out here!"

I managed to get in front of Isaiah, but we were all distracted by my dad. "Bando?" I heard Isaiah say to himself.

Ms. Tia emerged from the house and it looked like she saw a ghost when she laid eyes on Ace or Bando or whoever he was.

"Damn, sis. You having a family get together and don't even invite your brother?" It seemed like the only people shocked about Ms. Tia's revelation were me and Isaiah. I watched my father for a reaction and he didn't have one.

"Can someone tell me what the fuck is going on?" Isaiah shouted.

"You was really about to trip with your uncle, nephew?" Ace smirked.

"Nephew?" Keisha commented as I saw her and Shawnie coming from the pool house.

I was ready to shit bricks, because there was no way I was letting Isaiah's uncle rub on my pussy. *This is not it, Jesus. Miami can't be this fucking small. I couldn't catch a break to save my life.*

I had never seen Ms. Tia in this state. She always seemed confident and in control, but not right now. I watched my dad slide Ms. Tia behind him and take control of the situation.

"Bando, I'm not going to disrespect Tia because you are her baby brother. But you need to go. You ain't welcomed here. Nobody wants you here."

"Jaya wants me here!" I think I peed a little as everybody's eyes were on me.

"Umm...see what happened was, umm, Ace, I mean Bando been helping me with my real estate license and he ummm, he... I'm just trying to do better for my daughter and I..I..." I rambled on.

"We decided that we wanted to be together." Ace snatched me by the hand. "And we been fucking for a few months now." My mouth dropped from shock. I knew this nigga didn't just lie like that. I didn't have a chance to react because Isaiah was taking off on Ace.

My dad and Shawnie raced to break up the fight, and once they got Isaiah somewhat calm, I tried to talk to him.

"There ain't shit you got say to me, Jay!"

"I'm not fucking him!"

"Something went down though."

I diverted my eyes because the guilt was all on my face. "That night your mom got shot, I thought you was out cheating and Ace popped up to take me out. I was drunk and—"

"You fucked him?"

"No. But we came close. But I left—"

"I told you the nigga wanted to fuck and you still was entertaining this nigga. You always assuming shit. But you ain't got to assume shit now. I'm done with you." Isaiah pushed past my dad and me to go back in the house. I saw that Shawnie had made Ace leave. Ace took one look at Shawnie and knew he didn't want them problems.

"Isaiah?" My eyes got teary. "Isaiah!" I tried to reach for him, but the look in his eyes when he turned around to face me had me stumbling back. If looks could kill, I would have been dead.

"Baby, I only want you."

"The fucked up thing was that I been nothing but faithful. My mom gets shot and you go smash my uncle? Yup, I'm good." Isaiah walked off.

"I didn't know he was your uncle. Shit, you didn't know he was your uncle."

"And that makes it better?"

"No! I didn't fuck him!"

"The fact that it took only a few hours of me not answering the phone for the next nigga to get a chance, lets me know you don't love me."

"That's not true!" I cried so hard as I tried to grab Isaiah. But he snatched away from me. "Isaiah!"

"Let him go." My dad stopped me from chasing after Isaiah.

I real life broke my own heart. I hurt the man that had never done me dirty. I had put him through hell from the moment I came back to Miami. Maybe I didn't deserve happiness, because I was always fucking up shit. I was like that retarded dude from that Martin Lawrence movie, *Life*. Can't Get Right.

✦ 17 ✦

BANDO

"**M**r. Collins, you would be so proud of all the homes I sold today." I popped my head into my boss' office.

"That's good, Ace," Mr. Collins responded warmly. "I got an investor call in fifteen minutes, but I got some personal matters to handle. Could you hop on the call?"

"I got you, Mr. Collins," I confirmed as I went back to my own office to prepare for the investor call.

My relationship with my family was fucked up. My relationship with the woman I loved was fucked up. But as far as my work life, shit was Gucci. Mr. John Collins had given me a position as part-time janitor when I first got out of the Northeast Florida State Hospital in MacClenny. But he saw my drive to do more than clean toilets. So in the past seven months, I'd been promoted to business partner. I got my real estate license and it was up from there. I appreciated Mr. Collins for giving me a chance, because most people wouldn't.

After the investor call, my bae was heavily on my mind, so I called her.

"What are you doing?"

"Who is this?"

"I got a new number. It's Ace."

"I told you not to call me anymore." Jaya got hostile.

"But—"

"Nah, nigga. That shit you pulled at Ms. Tia's was uncalled for. We ain't fuck. We ain't together."

"So you going to really tell yourself that you don't want me?"

"Hell no. Don't fucking call me no more." And just like that, the phone call ended.

I smiled to myself because Jaya had me intrigued, and her ass knew what she was doing. I was hooked. She was a loyalist. Jaya wanted to be with me but my nephew was in the way. *Baby, don't even worry, I'ma take care of all that.*

I had a showing for a home in French County Village and needed to go. I saw that Mr. Collins was on a call, so I did a quick head nod and got to my car.

I wished my mom could see how good I had turned out despite Tia turning her back on me. Not only had she turned her back on me, but she was fucking the opp. Tia knew that Jayson killed my dad, and yet she was over there playing house with the nigga. I was going to fall back and not bring no smoke her way. And when she asked me to fall back from hitting Ice's spots, I did out of respect. Because even after she left me in the state hospital by myself, she still was my sister. I wanted us to build up something because her and her kids were my only family. But she chose sides, and so was I. She'd been dealing with Ace this whole time, but now I was going to have to show her how Bando got down. My list was getting longer. Up until that little barbecue my sister had, the only person I was out to kill was Jayson. But now I was going to add my sister and my nephew. But I didn't just want to kill Ice. I was going to take his daughter, his bitch, and I was back to hitting all his spots. Ace chose peace. But Bando was picking violence.

"Where you at?" I asked Rio as soon as he answered the phone.

"Dropping off my kids. Why, what's up?" Gio's brother asked. Even though I sold houses, my main job was selling drugs because when I first got out, being a part-time custodian wasn't about to cut it. I had to get to the bag. I didn't have the means to buy no work. But I got my hands on a gun and learned how to use it. So I was robbing niggas for their corners and work. I took what I wanted and I was good at it.

"This nigga Ice is about to feel this wrath. Hit all his spots. Don't even take the dope or the money. Burn them muthafuckas down! This is for Gio."

"I'm with it. I'll hit you when I'm done."

I felt a little better now that Ice was going to see that I wasn't to be fucked with. I let him think that bulldagger had killed me. They didn't know what I looked like, so when they killed my boy, Devin, I fell back. If anything, it was Tia's idea. She wanted to play like I was the evil one, but we were both the fruit of the same poisonous tree. She had done worse than me. She may not have killed the nigga that was beating on her mom, but she had killed way more than me. And if I was going down, I'd bring her bougie ass with me. Everybody was going to find out her secrets.

I wasted no time as I pulled up to the house I was trying to sell. I got out the car and let Bando fade into the abyss of my mind and let Ace, the businessman, take center stage. I had eight prospective clients coming to the house, so I rushed to lay out some cookies and cigars for the clients. I barely had the cookies on the tray before my first client came in.

"This is a beautiful home." The woman smiled as she looked around.

"I've already had five offers," I lied. The house just went on the market this morning, but she didn't need to know that. "But you see why. The house has four bedrooms, three full bathrooms, two half baths. Over a thousand square feet in storage and closet space. The home has a vintage wine cellar and covered pool." I listed some of the house's qualities.

"My husband would love something like this."

"Yes, he would. Here, let me give you a quick tour...."

"Dejahnae Mitchell."

"Alright, Mrs. Mitchell, let's start by the front door so you can see the craftmanship of the foyer alone." Dejahnae followed as I led the way.

18

KEISHA

"I don't think we should invite any of them. I don't want that negative energy around us," I commented as I laid my head on Shawnie's chest. Shawnie's birthday was coming up and we both wanted to have a party. But we weren't sure if we wanted Jaya and Ice to be in attendance. My man's birthday was a time for love and a good time. And because he was family, I knew that neither of them would be mature enough to put their differences aside like adults.

"I know," Shawnie replied but was texting away on his phone. I was trying to peek to see who it was. "You want to read it?" Shawnie and I made eye contact.

"Boy, nobody cares that you checking up about your big dick cream you ordered." I insulted Shawnie because he caught me being nosy.

"But you be choking on it. Anyways, that's my sister and my bro. I'ma holler at them about it though." I saw that Shawnie didn't want to talk about it anymore, so I dropped it. "Baby, you know we ain't got to do all this. I already got my birthday present." Shawnie caressed my body, sending shivers down my spine.

"What the fuck ever, nigga!" I rolled my eyes, but I was smiling. All the bullshit and me and Shawnie were together.

"When we fight, can't let the world know
Don't tell a groupchat or let your girls know
They be happy to see you down
They be happy to see you down
And my heart cold but you heat it up
Get you to the crib, lick it, beat it up
Real power couple winning, can't compete with us," I began to rap.

"Not that song, babe."

"Why?"

"It was me and Dejah's song."

I just stared at him, but I knew my anger was in my eyes and all over my face. My ass was hot.

"I guess." I tried to sit up, but Shawnie hurried and snatched my ass up.

"We already got a song. "

"What song?" I looked at Shawnie.

"Baby hit this weed 'cause it might calm you down
I rub your feet listenin' to everything you talkin' 'bout
Straight out the streets, I'm grimy
I talk, my diamonds shiny
Don't mean to be too aggressive baby
I go to war with God behind you
One thing I really love is makin' love to the pussy..." Shawnie rapped in my ear as he wrapped his arms around me.

And my mind flooded to right before Shawnie was going to prison and this was our song. Especially when I was mad. This song was me all the way. I would be going off wanting to fight everybody. But Shawnie knew that a blunt and some head would put me in a better mood. Or we would ride around all day doing drops and this was one of the songs that would be playing in the background as he rubbed his hand in between my legs.

"This was our song." I smiled "Can I ask you something? Is you in this for real or you just don't like to lose?"

"Lose what?"

"Lose me."

"A nigga was functioning on pain. I was hurt by you being with Tommy and I wanted to hurt you too. But I had to step back and realize what I really want. I figured if I was tripping with you it would keep you in the picture. But I see that wasn't enough for me. I had to grow up and see what I really want. And that's you. I'm done playing games. You don't miss Mr. Bernard?"

I knew his ass didn't ask me that bullshit. I left my fiancé at the altar, of course I was over him.

"No. I don't want him or miss him.."

"Ok, then you know that I don't miss Deja either. I'm in this shit ten toes down."

"You better, nigga."

"Can you get me some water, babe?"

"Why can't you get it your damn self? This is your house."

"Please?"

"You got me fucked up, if you think I'm about to be Molly the Maid." I got up from the bed.

"Thank you, bae."

"Kiss my ass!" I stomped off to the kitchen.

As soon as I stepped into the living room, I was taken aback. There were huge marquee letters that read, Keisha Marry Me. The ceiling was filled with white and macron pink helium balloons. There was a white runner that was placed from the marquee letters to where I stood with silver and white flower petals. The runner was lined with vases of flowers and LED candles. Pink peonies and white hydrangeas were so beautiful. And Shawnie knew they were my favorite. I ain't going to lie, my ass was ugly crying because I dreamed of this moment since I was a little girl. And not with just anybody, but with Shawnie.

"This is our real song." Shawnie came up behind me as "Ring" by Ye Ali played.

"You know it's all entertainment (yup)
Some people wanna be famous

I just keep it low, and stack this paper (I count it up)
And roll blunts with my baby, yeah
Ring, ring, ring, ring (hit me up)
Baby, I could be your private thing (brrp, brrp)
Show you things you ain't never seen (never seen)
We can keep it 'tween you and me
Ring, ring, ring, ring..."

The Kevin Gates ballad he sang to me earlier was our ride or die song. But "Ring" was our love song. And Shawnie really remembered.

"When did you pull this off?" I looked at the beauty of everything.

"When I was texting about my big dick cream I ordered." Shawnie and I both laughed.

Shawnie got on one knee. His ass was wearing nothing but some boxers, but it went well with the boy shorts and sports bra I was wearing. "The moment I saw you for the very first time back when we was kids will be stuck into my memory till the end of days, because it was the day when the course of my life radically changed its direction. I remember you coming to play with Jaya that first day after kindergarten. Getting on my damn nerves. You said one day I was going to be your baby daddy. And I remember thinking this girl is tripping. But over the years, I became more than that. Your protector. Your best friend. And the only woman I want to be with. You my entire heart, Kesh.

"I was so nervous to ask you to be my girlfriend when we was thirteen and fifteen years old. I have killed for you and I will do that shit again because I'ma always be your protector. We been through so much shit together. Selling drugs together. Going to jail together. Losing our virginity together. I took that dope case because I would be damned if I let you sit in a prison cell. I know you was going to do that time with me, but I fucked up, Kesh. I shouldn't have been entertaining no bitch. I can't say it enough, but I'm sorry for hurting you. My family loves you. They saw that we were meant to be before I knew it.

"I do not know how it has been possible to live without your love and your motivation, without listening to you singing and watching you dancing when you think nobody sees. The way you bring light to my world is a trip. I love dreaming with you because you understand me as nobody would ever understand.

"You encourage me to get up every morning, to do things, and to constantly become better. I went legit because of you. You are my inspiration, my motivation, and my desirous goal. You know like nobody what is happiness and where it is hidden. We both want to have a colorful and memorable life, and together we can make our dreams come true.

"I promise to do everything I can to be a perfect match for you and to become a husband you deserve. I want to become your happily-ever-after, and I will do my best for your incredible smile to never fade. You are the greatest and the most precious gift given to me by God. I know when he made you, he said this one is going to be for JaShawn.

"I am looking forward to the day when my last name will become yours, and our love will give a birth to a new family. You are the one I want to be with for better, for worse, for richer, for poorer. My voice is trembling, and my heart beats at a furious pace, since I hope you will say yes and make me the luckiest man on Earth. My heart, will you marry me?"

All I could do was shake my head up and down as Shawnie put on the ring I picked out over six years ago. The ring I saw in the mall and said that when we got married, this was the ring I wanted.

"I love you, JaShawn," I managed to say as our lips came together.

"I love you more, Kesh."

Shawnie's ass was full of surprises today. Because by the time nightfall hit, we were having an engagement announcement party. How this nigga know I was going to say yes? But Shawnie knew me because he knew that even though I didn't have my own family, his family had become my own. And the Mitchell family loved them some Keisha.

"I want to give a toast..." Mama Key stood up from the outside patio table on the veranda. Everybody got quiet and mirrored her by holding up their glass. "I want to say, first and foremost... It's about damn time!" Everyone erupted in laughter. "I love Keisha like she is my own daughter. I know you can't pick who your kid ends up with, but Keisha is my only pick. I want JaShawn happy with a woman that loves him, supports him, and is going to get in his ass when he's fucking up. Please join me in wishing the future JaShawn and Keisha Mitchell a prosperous marriage of love and many grandbabies!"

Everyone in attendance cheered. I looked around the backyard of everyone here and was so overwhelmed with love. JaShawn, Mama Key, Jaya, Jayson, Ms. Tia, Ice, the twins, Lil' Way, and Shanice. I knew that Shanice was Dejah's friend. She had a stank look on her face, but she didn't address me with no bullshit. If the roles were switched and I had to watch Jaya's man making plans for the future with another bitch, I would be hot too. So that's why I didn't press the issue too much. But bitches knew not to hop in my face.

Jaya and Ice had managed not to come to blows and I would forever be grateful. I could see it in her face how hurt she was about her and Ice breaking up. "You alright, best friend?" I draped my arm around Jaya.

"No. This nigga got me blocked and communicates through Ms. Tia or my dad to get Israel." Jaya bounced Israel and smiled at her daughter. "Bitch, I done broke down and bought me a rose, a dildo, and a massager."

"I'm about to throw my phone." I giggled. "Bitch, I know you lying."

"Girl, the shit got me fiening like a crackhead. I damn near was ready to take Hank out on a date."

"Who is Hank?"

"The dildo," Jaya whispered. "But a dildo can't cuddle or go with me to my prenatal appointments."

"You're pregnant?" I was so excited.

"Yeah," Jaya grumbled.

"Does Ice know?"

"Yeah, his bitch ass knows. This nigga going to say, 'Why the fuck you telling me? Tell your baby daddy.' Bitch, I was hot and that's why I slashed all his tires. My body count is still at two. Well, three if you want to count Hank. But as far as human-to-human sex, it's still two. I keep telling him I didn't fuck his uncle, but he ain't trying to hear it. Talking about he glad his grandpa is dead because I would try to fuck him too. This nigga really trying to play me like I'm some hoe. At this point, what is ten minus six?"

"Umm, four..." I didn't know where this was going.

"The streets! That's what I'm about to be. Me and Hank about to be outside. Don't look at me like that. You know I'm too damn scary to be a hoe. I'm talking all this shit knowing damn well my revenge is about to be getting the bag."

"I don't know why we both can't be happy at the same time. This some bullshit," I honestly replied. I wanted my best friend happy with me so we could go on double dates and shit. But mainly because Jaya could have fucked Ace but she chose to be faithful. I swear niggas couldn't take it when a female did them how they did us.

"I'm not even tripping. I'm happy for you and Shawnie—"

"Can I have everybody's attention?" Everybody turned to see Dejah standing by the back fence. "I have some words for the happy couple too."

"Dejah, come on." Shawnie tried to usher Dejah into the house.

"No! I'm the wife. You are not going to push me into the

darkness. How you proposing marriage but you still married, JaShawn?"

"Don't do this shit right here—"

"We going to do it here. Because everybody needs to know that you left your pregnant wife to play house with a stripper."

The old me would have popped off, but she was hurt, and instead of trying to confront her, I sat my ass down.

"The right thing to do would have been your family saying, JaShawn, go back to your wife. But noooo! They throw a party to celebrate adultery. But why should I be surprised? Y'all all trifling. Jaya fucking her sister's man. Keyonna think she still is twenty-five. And your uncle just got out of jail for drugs."

"Chill the fuck out!" Shawnie got loud.

"I'ma go. But just know you will never see your daughter." It seemed like the world slowed down to a standstill. Everyone watched in terror as Dejah pulled a gun out her purse. She aimed the gun at Shawnie before turning the gun on herself.

"Noooo!" I tried to run over to them, but by the time I took three steps, Dejah had the gun pressed against her stomach. I watched helplessly as Dejah pulled the trigger.

Pow

Blood flew everywhere, and Dejah dropped to the ground. I felt nothing but guilt and pity. I wanted nothing in this world but to be with Shawnie. But not at the cost of someone's life. Everyone was screaming and I froze up. I stood with a thousand tears streaming down my face. All I could do was pray that both of them would be okay. If I would have stayed away from Shawnie, none of this shit would have happened. Dejah was unresponsive on the ground. I doubt if the baby lived. Poor baby, she didn't deserve to die. I prayed for Dejah and her daughter's safety, but there wasn't enough prayer in the world to cleanse this guilt.

What the fuck have I done?

❧ 19 ❧

ICE

Lil' Way rolled up the blunt as me and my two friends sat in silence, caught up in our own thoughts and problems. You would have thought that my mom's love life was what was bothering me, but it wasn't. There had been a string of fires in the vicinity of a lot of my trap houses. And it didn't take rocket science to know it was none other than Bando trying to hit my spots. This nigga was really ready to die behind a bitch I no longer wanted. He could have Jaya's friendly ass, I was good on her.

I knew her ass didn't cheat, but it was the principle of while I'm checking on my OG you dry humping the next nigga. All she had to say was she wasn't happy and I would have kicked rocks. Because there was no way in hell she would have entertained another man if she was happy in our relationship. I should have known when she got that Rent-A-Center couch shit was sus.

Everything in me wanted to cut her ass off financially. And the only reason I didn't was because she had my daughter. Israel didn't play about her daddy. She didn't say "mama," her word was "dada." And at ten months old, she would be so hyped when I walked in the door. Her ass was even starting to look like me. Everywhere we would go, people swore up and down she was my twin. Not one drop of blood that ran through Israel was mine, but that was my daughter and nothing or no one could change that.

"How's the baby?" I asked Shawnie. It had been ten days since Dejah had shot herself in the stomach, but Shawnie's daughter, Jenesis, was a fighter. She was currently in ICU at only two pounds, born via c-section.

"She's a fighter. She on a breathing and feeding tube, but she's getting better every day. I know when I see Dejah, I'ma dead that bitch. And that's on my mama."

In the midst of the commotion of Dejah shooting herself, Shawnie took the gun and cleaned Dejah's hands before the police came. He had everybody agree to the story of a stray bullet hitting Dejah. He understood that Dejah wasn't thinking correctly, and he only blamed himself because he had left her pregnant. But since Dejah had been discharged from the hospital, she had yet to visit her daughter. And while no one wanted to admit it out loud, we all knew Dejah meant to kill Jenesis.

"Bro, me and Shanice is here for you no matter what." Lil Way lit the blunt.

"I appreciate it," Shawnie commented back. "You taking on extra shifts so I can be with my daughter helps a lot, zo."

Here came Jaya calling from her auntie Key's number, and I ignored that shit. I hit the blunt a few times and hit the streets. I had my own blunt in the car, so I lit that muthafucka up and rode around nowhere particular.

The blunt had me hungry, so I stopped at this little barbecue place in the Gardens. I was waiting for my food when I saw this bad ass bitch walk up to the food truck I was standing at. I wasn't looking to be with nobody, but shit, if Jaya was for the streets, then so was I. I didn't want to hang out with no bitches, but I didn't mind getting my dick wet.

Me and the baddie made eye contact. She was a bold one and approached me. "I'm Luz. What's your name?"

I licked my lips as I took in this Spanish chick's beauty. That ass was fat and I imagined how I was going to have her bent over before the night was over. "I'm—"

"Taken!" Jaya came out of nowhere. How the fuck she knew where I was at? "Did he tell you he has two kids and one on the way?" Jaya rubbed her flat stomach. "You seem like a nice girl. You willing to get your ass beat behind him?" Jaya stepped forward and mami stepped back. She didn't waste any time getting the fuck from over here.

"You ain't my bitch! Move around, Jay!" I had lost interest in the food and the bitch I was trying to holler at. There was no way I could fuck with a bitch that was going to be scary. If some shit popped off, the bitch was snitching about any fucking thing. I began to walk back to my car, but Jaya was on my heels.

"Why you ignoring my calls, Isaiah?"

"Because I don't have shit to say to you." Jaya jogged to block the driver's side door to prevent me from getting inside my car. "Move."

"How many times you want me to apologize? I miss you, babe. I want to come home. I want to get married to you."

"I think it's too late for that shit. We co-parenting and that's it."

Jaya grabbed both sides of my face and kissed me like her life depended on it. The shit felt good, but shit wasn't about to change between us. "Go home, Jaya." I broke our kiss.

"Only if you coming with me," Jaya cried.

"Save your tears for that nigga." I was heartless.

"I don't want him. I only want you. I messed up, Isaiah. How long you going to hold that over my head? That whole incident with Bando made me realize how much I was taking for granted. I was trying to tell you what I did before he showed up."

"Yeah, whatever." I looked around at my surroundings before my eyes fell back on Jaya. "That relationship shit is dead, but I'm down to fuck." I let my hand caress Jaya's ass.

Jaya's face went from sadness to shock to anger. "Fuck you!" Jaya yelled out.

And all I could do was chuckle. "If you ain't about to let me hit it in the backseat of this truck, then move." I was dead ass serious and it showed in my face.

"I would never do you like this, Ice. You really going to treat me like some hoe?"

"Ain't that what you been showing me? I got some shit to do, go be for the streets like you been doing. And stop begging for a nigga to fuck with your hoe ass."

I saw I had pressed some buttons, and Jaya began to punch me in the face. I was never the woman beater, but ask Trinity, and I could go from Isaiah Green to Chris Brown in a hot second. I choke slammed Jaya against my car.

"Bitch, you got me fucked up!" I got in Jaya's face. "You worried about the wrong shit." I shoved my finger in her forehead. "I ain't fucking with you." I finally let go and Jaya sobbed like a little baby. I ain't gonna lie, I didn't want to put hands on her because I did still love her. But if I was going to move on, I couldn't entertain any possibilities of us being together.

"I'm pregnant. Why would you do that!"

Damn, I forgot that fast that Jaya was pregnant. I was currently denying I was the daddy, but I knew that was my baby. I was doing Jaya super dirty by not going to none of the appointments. And I had to realize that my anger was affecting my unborn too.

"I'm sorry." I quickly kissed Jaya's forehead.

"Don't touch me." Jaya wiped where I kissed her and began to walk back to her car. "If it ain't about Israel, you ain't got to worry about me contacting you again," Jaya said over her shoulder.

"What about the baby?" I called out.

"It's not yours, remember?"

I wasn't built to be an asshole like Shawnie. I grabbed for Jaya and she snatched away from me, but I wasn't letting up and wrapped Jaya in a bear hug. She fought me at first, but then her ass began to cry. My shirt was drenched in her tears as I whispered sorry for treating her like a hoe.

"I'm sorry." Jaya kissed me again. "I'm sorry, Isaiah."

Emotions were high as I opened Jaya's mouth with my tongue. The heat that dispersed between us was hotter than a ninety-degree day in Miami. "Follow me to my house." I broke our kiss.

We barely made it past the front door before I had Jaya butt ass naked and hitting it from the back. Her pussy was feeling just like when she was pregnant with Israel. I was about to beat the pussy up as I spread Jaya's ass cheeks to slip deeper in. Our skin was slapping together as Jay moaned how much she loved me.

"Fucccck!" I grunted as I nutted.

Jaya rolled to her side and looked at me. "I didn't cum."

"Okay." I shrugged as I located my jeans and put them back on. "Whatchu about to do?"

"Nigga, I know you better quit playing with me." Jaya wrapped her arms around my neck as my hands fell on her bare ass. "I'm not about to beg you, Isaiah. We together or not?"

"I'm tired of the games. So you tell me."

"We gonna try this again."

I didn't think there was anyone on this Earth as toxic as me and Jaya. But that was bae, so we were going figure it out one way or another.

◈

"Can I holler at you?" I walked into the kitchen feeling like Jody from *Baby Boy* when he discovered Melvin had moved in.

It didn't help that Jayson had them prison muscles and his ass didn't have nothing on but some boxer briefs on, frying bacon.

"Yeah, what's on your mind—"

"You ready for round three?" My mom came prancing out her bedroom wearing nothing but a see-through robe, not hiding a damn thing.

"Ma?" I wanted to gouge out my eyes.

"Hey, Isaiah!" My mom wrapped her robe around her body, but it did little to cover her body or erase the images from my mind. "What are you doing here?"

"I came to holler at Jayson." I tried to look at anything but them. They were in their forties, so sex should be the last thing on their minds.

"Okay." My mom smiled. "I'ma be in the hot tub." My mom got on her tippy toes as Jayson slobbered her up.

It was the nastiest shit I had ever seen.

"I'ma holler at baby boy then I'm going to join you."

Baby boy? I drove my own car over here. And not a damn bike or my bitch's car. I wasn't even dark skinned like Jody. The fuck?

"Will you put my plate in the microwave?"

"I got you."

"Don't be long." My mom turned her attention to me as Jayson slapped her ass. "Don't forget about that drop today."

"T, lay off the boy. Let him be a man."

I was waiting for my mom to pop off, but she did the weirdest thing. "I know you got this, son." Who the fuck was this woman? Because this was not my mother, Tia Green. She didn't play about her money.

My mom looked at Jayson with lust as she grabbed a piece of bacon to eat. They stood there for hot second smiling all goofy at each other. I really think they forgot I was standing there.

"What?" My mom smiled hard as fuck.

"I can't believe we matured to this." Jayson kissed her forehead.

"I know." Ma Dukes switched off like her ass was grown and fucking. "I'll see you later, son."

"You know, after I broke your mother's heart, I tried to find someone just as good and no one came close. I didn't think I would have another chance." Jayson looked down the hall where my mom disappeared to. "Ain't no woman like your mama. She still got—"

"You don't have to share no more. I believe you."

"My bad. What you want to holler at me about?"

"Bando."

"I see. What's going on?"

"I want to kill this nigga."

"Is it because of Jaya?"

"Part of the reason. The nigga is real disrespectful."

"Your mama going to kill me for telling you this, but I think you should hear it. I was a fucked up nigga. Even worse than when I was in prison. I met your mom when I was twenty and she was fifteen. I fell in love with her the moment I saw her. I mean, she was bad, she still is. She got that timeless beauty. But it wasn't just that. She is my soul mate and I never met nothing damn near close. And I'm not trying to knock Jaya's mama, but my heart always belonged to Tia. But because I was so insecure about losing her I drug her through the mud. I did her so dirty and the only crime she did against me was that she loved me. That shit still fucks with me.

"You was supposed to be my son. But because I was doing your mama so dirty, she had a one-night stand with this Cuban man. All this time and some nigga she fucked only once gets her pregnant, I was heated. I never looked at why she was reacting the way she was, and I lost her. Until now. I'm learning to not get involved with you and Jaya's relationship. But I know her ass loves you just like you love her. I promise Bando wouldn't be acting like that if he had smashed. I want to kill that nigga too. But I can't hurt your mama like that. I know you want to get this nigga, but revenge is how I lost your mama the first time. You kill this nigga, and it's going to feel good for a hot second. But then you got to deal with your crazy ass mama. You see all the shit that's gone down? And this nigga still breathing. A lot of that is guilt because she feels she failed him. But talk to your mama first before you make a move. Alright?"

I soaked up everything Jayson said. I didn't know shit was that serious between him and

Ma Dukes, and I had more respect for my mother because despite all the shit she been through, she took care of me and my sisters. "Alright."

"But that don't mean don't give that nigga hell. Hit him where it hurts...in his pockets. Jaya said he got a real estate business. We going to get that nigga, don't even trip."

"Alright, bet." I slapped hands with Jayson.

"But just know that me and your mama don't have any secrets. So I'ma let her know what we doing. Is that cool?"

"Do you." I stood up to leave.

"Grab you a plate before you go. I'ma go see what your mama is talking about." Jayson made his way to the hot tub room.

How the fuck was I supposed to have an appetite to eat anything, knowing this nigga was about to be smashing my mama?

❧ 20 ❧

SHAWNIE

"Can I speak to Mr. JaShawn Mitchell?"

"Yes, this is him." I didn't know who was calling.

"Hi, my name is Crystal Marshall, I'm a nurse here at Jackson Memorial. I'm sorry to inform you, but your daughter has passed away."

I immediately got hostile. "What the fuck you mean she gone? I just came home to take a shower. I only been gone twenty minutes. The doctor said she was thriving."

"And she was. The problem is that she didn't die of natural causes."

"What the fuck is that supposed to mean?"

"The detective will inform you when you get here." I didn't say nothing else but hung up the phone. I told Keisha to get dressed and did 90 mph to get to Jackson Memorial.

As soon as I reached the NICU floor, muthafuckas were in my face. "Mr. Mitchell?"

"Yeah?"

"I'm Detective Coleman and I have been assigned to your daughter's case. Can we go somewhere to talk?"

I followed Detective Coleman to a family room and sat down with Keisha holding my hand. The whole ride here, the words unnatural causes had taken residence in my head. All kinds of scenarios played in what happened to my daughter.

"Approximately fifteen minutes after you left, Jenesis' mother came."

I could feel a knot in my stomach and it grew by the second. "Okay."

"Four minutes into the visit, Dejah purposely placed a breastfeeding pillow over Jenesis' face until she stopped breathing. Nurses found Jenesis on the floor, unresponsive. The nurses worked frantically to try to save your daughter, but it was too late." The detective coughed to keep from crying, but both me and Keisha were in tears. "Dejah did leave a letter. Do you know what this means?" Detective Coleman handed me Ziploc bag with a single piece of paper in it.

"You'll never play house with my baby. I'd rather her be dead than for you to have her around that bitch," read the note.

I was lost for words. This bitch killed my baby because of the next bitch. I knew I hurt Dejah. I knew I wasn't the best husband, but her ass didn't have to snap and kill our baby. I made sure to go to every appointment. If Dejah had cravings, I would get whatever she needed. More than anything, I tried to be her friend. I would have rather she kill me than kill Jenesis.

I just sat there and cried while Keisha held me. I noticed that someone opened the room door and stepped in with my baby girl. She was wrapped in a soft pink blanket and had on a big pink headband. Long gone were the tubes, and Jenesis looked so peaceful like she was sleeping. The only dead giveaway was that her body was cold and stiff.

"We are going to give you a moment." The detective and nurse spoke before exiting the room.

"This is all my fault." Keisha looked at me with tears pouring from her eyes.

"This isn't nobody's fault but Dejah's. Be mad at me, but don't kill our daughter." My eyes continued to mourn with tears.

We both turned our attention to Jenesis, Keisha laid her head on my shoulder and hummed.

"Please don't take my baby from me Kesh."

"I'm not going to get the abortion. Seeing your daughter lets me know that I have no right to choose who gets to be here and who doesn't."

"At this point, I don't want to know if I'm the father or not. The baby is mine."

"Okay." Keisha didn't argue, and that's what I loved about her. Her ass knew how to pop off, but she knew the right time and place for that shit. "This bitch really took my daughter. Dumb ass bitch, this was your daughter too. I'ma kill her, Kesh. That's on me. Scary ass bitch gonna take her pain out on an innocent child. I chalked up her shooting herself as she was going through some shit. That I hurt her and I needed to give her the benefit of the doubt. But this shit right here is unforgivable. I'm stomping that hoe out when I find her."

"And when you do, I will be your alibi."

ꙮ 21 ꙮ

DEJAH

"How is my daughter?" I asked Bando.

"They think you killed her."

"What?"

"The police. JaShawn. They all think you're baby killer. Here, look." Bando pulled out his phone and hit play.

"Tonight the city of Miami mourns the death of three-week-old Jenesis Mitchell. According to Dade County Police Department, Jenesis' mother, twenty-six-year-old Dejahnae Mitchell and estranged wife of JaShawn Mitchell, walked into Jackson Memorial and smothered her daughter. Leaving the infant child on the floor like trash. Dade County is asking the public to be on the lookout for Dejahnae, also known as Dejah. Dejah is described as an African American female..."

If my arms weren't tied up, I would have punched the shit out of Bando. "All I asked you was to check to see about my daughter," I screamed. Not too long after I got released from the hospital, Bando kidnapped me. Had me locked away in some garage. I was missing my daughter and wanted to make sure she was alright. I begged and pleaded with Bando to just check and see if she was okay. But instead, he dressed up like me and killed the only reason I had to live.

"Hey, you already didn't want her here when you shot your-self." Bando shrugged. "I just sent her where she needed to be."

"You know damn well that you drugged me with Seroquel. If I was in my right mind, I would not have shot my damn self."

"You know deep down you didn't want that baby. I just gave you the outcome you wanted."

I told Bando when I thought he was a real estate agent that I was feeling down that my husband left me and I was going to have to raise my daughter by myself. Nowhere in my statement did I say I wanted to kill Jenesis.

This nigga was crazy. He wanted to show me a house, so I met up with him. I complained that I had a headache and he gave me some "vitamins," and I didn't remember shit after that. I woke up in the hospital not pregnant and with my daughter in the NICU. Bando gamed me. He knew I was depressed, lonely, and desperate for human interaction. My daughter was only two days old when Bando invited me for coffee across the street from the hospital. Who knew that day would be the last day I saw Jenesis, or that I'd find out, in this very chair, tied up, that I was drugged when I shot myself.

"Wait till Shawnie finds out—"

"He already does. Who you think he wants to kill?" Bando removed the wig he was wearing. "The man he heard of, or his soon-to-be ex-wife that 'allegedly'"—Bando did air quotes with his hands—"went crazy and killed his daughter. So, I think that he don't want to see you."

I wanted to mourn my daughter, but I didn't have the luxury to since I was tied up to this chair and it seemed like Bando fed off my fear. I tried to remain calm, but my heart was aching for Jenesis. I couldn't believe Bando dressed up as me and killed my daughter. I was wondering why he shaved his beard and mustache this morning, and now I saw why. But how the fuck did no one notice that he was a man in a dress? No one ques-tioned shit? I was so confused on how he could walk up into the

SOMEONE TO CALL BAE 3

NICU, kill my baby, and walk out without so much as being questioned or apprehended.

"Just let me go. I don't even remember your real name," I lied. "Your beef ain't even with me."

"No, but it is with your husband's uncle. When I said I was coming for everybody associated with Jayson, I meant that shit. You seem like a nice lady. You really do. But you just happen to be in the wrong place at the wrong time. The upside is you and your daughter can see each other again."

And just like that, Bando told me I was going to die. The weird thing was, it didn't seem like such a bad idea. I was going to miss my mama, and I didn't want her to live with a broken heart since I was her only child. But other than my mama, I had nothing else to live for. The news portrayed me as a bitter wife that was willing to kill her daughter to get back at her husband for leaving her. I was sad, I may have even been bitter, but I would never bring harm to my own child.

I watched Jaya lose her mind when her daughter was kidnapped. I really couldn't see myself living in this world without my Jenesis. As a matter of fact, I didn't want to live without her. I had accepted that Shawnie didn't want me, he wanted Keisha. I was already dealing with a broken heart from my husband leaving me, and my daughter getting murdered sent me to the realm of insanity.

"Fuck it. Kill me, nigga!" I screamed as tears rolled down my face.

"See, that's what the fuck I'm talking about!" Bando got happy. I closed my eyes as Bando pressed the cold metal against my temple.

Click.

I was confused about why I was still here. I opened my eyes and Bando was still standing there. I was in this hot ass garage, but sadly, I was still alive. "You gonna die, Ms. Lady, but not today." Bando walked out of the garage, turned off the lights, and closed the door. Why was he toying with me? Just kill me already.

I was left in the darkness with my pain and grief, and to be honest, this shit was worse than death.

❧ 22 ❧

JAYA

"I zzy!" I cooed at my nephew as he took steps toward me. He and Israel were only a few weeks apart and he was already walking. But Israel wasn't far behind. My babies were getting so big, and I was here for it.

"I'm home!" I heard Ice walk in the door.

"I'm in here, babe!" I yelled from the den.

Ice bent down to kiss me and then kissed Izzy and Israel. "How was your day?"

"It was good. We went to the park, then your mom and my dad watched the kids so I could take the real estate exam. Came home and cooked dinner."

"How you think you did?"

"I don't know. The shit had me stressed."

"Baby, if I got to buy you a license, I will do that shit. "

"Thank you," I gushed.

"I gotta get in these streets tonight with your dad. You going to be alright?"

"Yes."

"See if Keisha can come over."

"She been staying close to home since Jenesis died. I don't blame her. Shawnie been on the war path."

"If I was him, I would too. I didn't even know Dejah was crazy."

"Shit, me either. She was always so sweet. But I guess when you snap, nothing is going to stop you from revenge. I just wish that she didn't take it out on the baby."

"Tomorrow, let's do something with them. Get them out the house. I hate seeing my nigga like this. When he catches up to Dejah, he's going to fuck her ass up!"

"Yeah, he is."

"What did you cook, babe?" Isaiah got up from the floor.

"Some chicken, veggies, baked macaroni and cheese, and some biscuits. Your plate is in the microwave."

"Damn, babe. I'ma smash this plate and hop in the shower before your dad pulls up."

As soon as Isaiah got in the shower, my dad was at the door. "Daddy, please don't let nothing happen to Isaiah," I greeted my dad.

"I got him. Plus, I made a promise to Tia I wouldn't hurt her brother."

"You be safe too, Daddy."

"What? You giving your dad another chance?"

"I guess." I rolled my eyes.

"I appreciate it. Them last months in prison, I was doing you and Isaiah wrong. I had my back against the wall with Bando and I was moving so reckless. And sadly, it took me losing your sister to realize how I was treating you. But I'm really trying to regain your trust."

"Okay." I acknowledged my father's efforts.

"You ready?" Isaiah came down the stairs behind me. "Alright, babe. I'll see you later."

I said bye to Isaiah and my dad. It was almost eight o'clock, so I stripped the babies down, gave them a bath and a warm bottle, and put them to sleep. I talked to Keisha while I cleaned up the kitchen, hopped in the shower, and was knocked by the time my head hit the pillow.

I was awakened by Isaiah taking a shower, but I was so tired I didn't move. "Baby, everything go okay?"

"Yeah! Your dad just dropped me off."

I nestled in the warmth of the covers, fighting to stay awake. Isaiah hopped out the shower and I could smell his favorite cologne all the way from the bathroom. I knew this nigga was going to want some pussy, but my ass was tired, even though my pussy was wet from anticipation. I played sleep as Isaiah turned off the light and crawled into the bed with me.

I didn't move as I let Isaiah dip his finger in my pussy. Then his nasty ass gonna suck my juices from his fingers.

"You're so fucking nasty." I giggled. I went to kiss Isaiah, and something wasn't right. It was complete darkness, but even in the dark I knew that whoever this man was, was not Isaiah. I froze up. I was butt ass naked and I was scared that I was so close to getting raped. I had to think fast for my next move.

"Don't forget I'm still mad at you, Isaiah." I snatched away in fake anger. The man reached for me, but I slapped his hand away. "Dick can't be the solution for everything. I'ma go get some water and when I come back, we going to talk." I got out the bed and found my robe.

My mind was racing on how I was going to get my kids and get out this house wearing nothing but a robe and no shoes. I only made it to my bedroom door before the man had grabbed me by my hair.

"Isaiah, stop!" I tried to keep up the charade.

The man quickly turned on the lights and made me face his wrath.

"Ace?" I stared in horror.

"Nope. Ace is a little busy." Ace tapped his temple with his index finger. "When Ace said you was the one, I thought the nigga was lying until I tasted the pussy for my damn self."

"Bando?"

"In the flesh, baby. Where's your daddy at?" Bando gripped my hair tighter.

"I don't know."

"Oh, you know."

"For this very reason, he don't tell me shit about what he does." I was so terrified.

"My nephew with him?"

"I don't know," I lied.

"Jaya, stop playing with me."

"I swear I don't know shit," I cried.

"Oh, you going to tell me." Bando began to fumble at my robe while simultaneously dragging me to the bed. I fought like hell, but I was no match for his strength.

"I really don't know where they went." I spoke the truth as my back hit the bed. I was scared for me and my babies. I had to hype myself up that no matter what happened in this room to not scream and wake up Israel and Izzy. Bando looked like he was possessed by the devil himself. I had no idea what he was capable of, and I wouldn't allow my mind to play out my kids' demise. I didn't think he even cared about my dad and Isaiah's whereabouts. He was on some other shit. I ain't never been raped before, but I guess there was a first time for everything.

🦋 23 🦋

ICE

"How many we got left?" Jayson asked me as we merged into traffic as we burnt down another one of Coral Bay Realty's properties.

"Shit, a lot. But we already hit like twenty."

"Let's hit the office then."

"Put the address into the screen," I instructed Jayson.

As soon as the map popped up, I was making my way to the office.

The building was small and the security was easy to get past. There was a keypad entry pad, so I pulled out the passcode reader to crack the code. It took only a few seconds for the door to open. As soon as the door opened, Jayson and I split up to see what we could find. I was hoping to come across some money, because as much as Bando had taken from me, it was only right that I take his bread.

"Isaiah, come here," Jayson called for me. I followed his voice.

"What the fuck is that smell?" I covered my nose and mouth with the back of my sleeve.

"Some guy named John Collins." Jayson picked up the name plate off the desk. "He's been dead for at least a few months."

"So this nigga don't own his own business?"

"I don't think so. Probably killed this man so that he could take over. Instead of torching this muthafucka, we gonna send the police to find this body. We going to take his money and freedom."

"Bet."

After making the phone call to twelve, I had Jayson drop me off at home. It was late as fuck, so I knew that Jaya was still sleep. I was exhausted, so I just wanted to take a quick shower and get into the bed.

As soon as I got in the bedroom, I saw movement coming from the bed. Like some rocking type shit. I got mad quickly, and I knew Jaya didn't have no nigga in my bed. I turned on the light and saw Jaya with her knees to her chest, laying on her knees and rocking.

"Baby what's wrong?" That's when I saw that her face was stained with tears.

"Bando came looking for you... I told him I didn't know where you was at. He forced me to the bed," Jaya cried. "I kept begging him to stop. Trying to fight him off."

I didn't want to say the word, but I needed to know what happened. "Did he rape you?"

"I'm sorry, Isaiah," Jaya sobbed. "I gave him access to the safe in exchange for him not raping me."

"Which safe, Jaya?" I had a total of five safes in the house. The most visible was a safe that held two hundred dollars.

"Don't be mad at me."

"Which fucking safe?"

"The one in the floor under our bed."

I could feel my eyes water. "No, babe. Please tell me you lying."

"I wish I was."

"Five hundred racks, my nigga? You gave away five hundred

racks? That was most of our money, Jay." I was mad and ready to kick Jaya's ass.

"You don't think I know that? But it was either that or rape. He was going to rape me, Isaiah."

"Fuck! I punched the wall, making Jaya jump. "That was everything." I had to realize that it wasn't Jaya's fault. I got on the bed and wrapped my arms around my baby as she sobbed into my chest. I wanted to cry too. I was happy that Jaya was alright, but it took me so much time to save up that money. But I couldn't be mad at Jaya. I could only imagine how scared she was.

"What happened?" I needed to know.

"I thought I heard you in the shower…"

I listened carefully as Jaya ran down the whole night, and the shit had me pissed. But what got me was that Bando had split personalities. Ace was the man who showed up at my mama's house, but it was Bando who broke into my house. Ace, Bando, whoever the fuck he wanted to be, days were numbered. I understood that he was Ma Dukes' brother, but all that didn't matter when he put my family in danger. I loved my mama, but if we had to go to war behind her bitch ass brother, then so be it.

✦ 24 ✦

JAYSON

"I'm not killing my brother!" Tia yelled at me.

"I'm not asking you to. I'ma do the shit my damn self." I hit my chest.

"Your son can't even come to you about this shit because you've made the choice to protect your brother. He tried to rape my daughter last night, T. He took all your son's money. Look, I respected your decision before, but I can't anymore. I'm not trying to be funny, but I really didn't know Trinity, her mother didn't bring her around, so her death didn't impact me like it would if it was Jaya. Jaya is the only daughter I have left. You know how I feel about my daughter, and I'm killing Bando." I stood up from the bed.

"You giving me an ultimatum?" Tia got in my space.

"Why should I have to though? Your son couldn't reup if he wanted to. This nigga broke into the house and the only reason he didn't rape Jaya was because she gave him the money. But what if he did? She's pregnant with your grandbaby. I can't—"

"Okay! Okay! He's my brother, I will do it myself. But Jayson, you act like you didn't used to do shit."

"Oh, I was trying to rape pregnant bitches? I got split

personalities? Yeah, I was Ike Turner, but I wasn't no damn Ted Bundy."

Tia swallowed hard.

"I promise if this was Indica or Isis, you wouldn't be saying this bullshit."

"That's not true. I already feel bad that I wasn't there for him."

"Because the nigga been crazy." I bypassed Tia so I could leave.

"Where you going?" Tia questioned.

"I'm far from being a broke nigga. I'm here in this house because I love you. I love your girls and your son is like my son. But I'm not about to stay under the same roof with someone who is okay that her brother tried to rape my pregnant daughter."

"I love Jaya too. I told you I would kill him. What else do you want me to do?"

"Admit that it was Bando that shot you! Admit that he been a killer since he was a kid. Did he not strangle the neighbor's kittens? The crazy hospital only made him a patient and meticulous killer. It didn't cure him. The nigga has a dead body sitting in that real estate office. He couldn't get better if he wanted to. I'm not losing another daughter, T."

"I don't want to fight with you." Tia got in my space again. "I'm on your side. I said I'm giving the green light." I watched Tia tear up. I knew this was hard for her. I didn't care how much of a goon someone was, it was hard to kill someone you loved.

25

TIA

"I need to holla at you."

"Tia, do I look like I'm stupid? You gonna let the nigga that killed my dad tell you to kill me?"

"You tried to rape Jaya?"

"That's what she told y'all? Her ass been trying to throw me the pussy. We went out to dinner. She came to my house. I was in her house taking showers and shit. But I'm a rapist? She gave me that money because she wants to be with me!"

I couldn't let my brother twist the narrative. He was moving reckless and he was going to destroy everyone and everything around me if I let him. I saw he wasn't going to make this easy. I wasn't above killing nobody, but my brother had me feeling sick.

"Ace—"

"I got to go." Ace hung up the phone.

"Ma!" I heard Isis yelling for me.

"What, girl!" I came out my bedroom to find Isis holding a huge bouquet of flowers.

"You got a side piece?" Isis questioned.

"Where did these flowers come from?"

"They were just delivered." Isis pulled the card from the flowers and began to read.

Face down, ass up

Back, back, back it up

Lemme get both of them legs

And put 'em both behind your head

This shit is gettin' deep, deep up in there

Feel your legs gettin' weak up in here

Get a face full of that gushy, I'm close baby don't push me, this is how it always should be when

When we fuck..." Isis read. "Eww. Ma, please tell me that you are not being nasty?" Isis scrunched up her face.

"Mind your business!" I snatched the card and I smiled, because I now knew that Jayson sent the flowers.

"You been acting real grown lately. Is Jayson about to be our new stepdaddy or what?"

"Do you like him?" I wanted to know how my kids felt about Jayson. I knew that he and Isaiah were good, but I didn't know if my girls felt the same way.

"He's cool. He don't give me R. Kelly vibes. What I like about him the most is that you have had this smile since you got shot. Plus, he got money. He's gonna buy me and Indica a car."

"A car? You don't need another car. If you want a new car, you going to have to get a job and buy you one."

"But nobody around here has a job," Isis pouted.

"Isis, I'm about to snatch all them box braids out your head. Find you something to do. Do you see your punk ass daddy doing shit? And selling drugs is a job. Shit, it's a career move."

"Ma, drugs are not...nevermind. Can I have some money?"

"Why? I don't have a job."

"Ma! Stop playing. We both know I'm the only child that don't give you any problems. Can you please give me some money?"

"Actually, it's Indica that don't give me no problems."

"That's because she's basic."

"If she basic, so are you. Y'all literally got the same face."

"Ma? Everybody know I'm your best looking kid. Fine, you

don't have to give me no money. I'ma ask Jayson when he gets home."

"Don't be asking no man for no damn money. I suggest you get a job, Isis. I got some shit in motion and I got to give your brother some money. So money is tight."

"Ugh!" Isis stormed off. I didn't care about her attitude. Now I had to cover Ice's reup and replenish his stash. Today was about to be a long day. I didn't have trap houses, I had warehouses and apartments that housed my wealth.

"Babe! Get up." I woke Jayson up, who had been mad at me. "Thank you for the flowers."

"What flowers?" Jayson sat up, revealing the bareness of his chest. Looking all sexy and shit.

"You know you sent the flowers." Jayson pulled me onto the bed. "Get up! So we can get this money."

"I thought you was going to thank me for the flowers." Jayson kissed me.

"Later. Get up!" I got off the bed.

Jayson and I were dressed within the hour. It was crazy how I trusted Jayson with everything. And I wasn't the type of bitch to do shit like that. But getting shot showed me that we weren't our past, because Jayson stayed with me day and night until I recovered. I watched Jayson give the doctor fifty racks for saving my life. And even though he basically moved in with me, I never had to pay for shit. He really never stopped selling drugs when he went to prison. We didn't have the same territories, so I didn't have to worry about mixing business with pleasure.

Jayson pulled up to the Red Road Commons Apartments, the location I gave him. I owned two apartments under an LLC in this apartment complex. I had at least ten million in two apartments, but neither of these apartments was one of those. I loved my man, but I wasn't about to reveal my whole bag. The only one who knew about those two apartments were me and Jesus.

I had a million in each apartment here at the Red Road Commons. I just needed to empty one of the safes, which would cover everything Isaiah needed. This was a quick run of grabbing the money and giving it to my son.

"After this, let's go to the beach." Jayson stood behind me as I used my key to open the door of apartment of B-417.

I imagined laying on the beach as a sea breeze blew through my hair. Renting a cabana and getting felt on by my man. I had a few pieces I would fuck every now and then, but the bag was my man. Jayson had me spoiled since I wasn't used to dating since I was with the twins' daddy. I felt like I was young again and there was a glow that was undeniable, all because of Jayson Mitchell.

"Okay." I tried not to smile.

I could see the proudness in Jayson's eyes as he took in the realness of the apartment.

"Okay, T. I see you. I taught you well." Jayson kissed my forehead. I didn't know shit about selling drugs until Jayson had me cutting up coke and turning a profit. "My baby out here being a real queen pin."

Before Jayson and I broke up in the past, he got me into how to hid money and cocaine. And the first thing he taught me was how to have at least two apartments for such reasons. I took the knowledge and ran with it, because I had over ten apartments in the city. If I died tomorrow, my kids were set.

I followed Jayson as he looked around and pinpointed how good I hid the safes. We ended up in the bedroom and got distracted.

"Stop…" I moaned as Jayson pulled the gun I had hidden in my bra.

"You came prepared?" Jayson smirked as he held up my gun.

"So did you." I patted the gun in Jayson's waistband.

Jayson didn't respond as he traced the cold metal down my collar bone, between my breasts, and down my stomach.

"If this was a year ago, I think I would have blown your head off, T." Jayson's eyes turned dark.

"Nigga, I wouldn't have let you get that close though."

"But you have." Jayson put the gun on the nightstand before following the same pattern he traced with my nine with kisses.

"Who said that I don't want to still kill you?" I stared at Jayson, pulling the gun from his waist so quick and pointing it at his forehead.

Jayson smiled. "You want me dead, T? Pull the trigger." It seemed like eons as we stared each other down.

Jayson grabbed the gun I was holding and put it next to mine. As soon as he did, our mouths were connecting as I could feel Jayson lifting me up to take off my panties. I didn't know how I went to from hating him to loving him. My kids loved him and I felt protected in his presence.

"I should have shot your ass." I nibbled on Jayson's lip.

"But you not." Jayson had found my moist opening. "You love me too much."

"We fuck buddies. I don't love you." Jayson chuckled because he knew I was lying.

"Tell me you love me, T." Jayson slammed into me with so much velocity that I was cumming.

I love you, Jayson," I sang out as my whole body shook with orgasmic bliss. I hadn't even caught my breath as Jayson flipped me over onto my knees.

"I love you too." Jayson kissed my back before reminding me of how good dick had you acting. He brought a tsunami to the desert, and I was here for it.

I did not want to leave this bed, but I had to get this money to my son. I had showered and was waiting on Jayson to finish getting re-dressed. While Jayson was getting ready, I had stuffed a million dollars into a large duffle bag.

"Babe, let's rent a cabana," I yelled out as I zipped up the duffle bag.

"Okay. I'm starving. Book us a table at Ocean Prime." Jayson emerged from the bedroom still looking sexy.

I slid my phone to unlock it to reserve a table now since Ocean Prime was a new restaurant and everybody and their mama was going. Me and Jayson been wanting to try it, and my mouth was watering thinking of some crab legs.

"What—" My words got caught in my throat.

"Baby, you alright?" Jayson managed to say as Ace pressed his gun at the back of Jayson's head.

"You really fucking the opps, sis? This nigga was whooping your ass and killed my daddy. And yet you still let this nigga pipe you down?'

"Bando, this beef ain't got nothing to do with Tia. Just let her go," Jayson pleaded with my brother.

"Oh, y'all in love, love. You love him, Tia?"

"Y...yes," I told my truth. I wasn't a soft bitch, but a tear escaped my eye. I didn't think I could love someone as much as I loved my kids. But I was praying that both me and Jayson were going to be able to walk out of here.

"You know, when I shot you, I wasn't trying to shoot you, sis. I was trying to shoot your little boyfriend."

"Bando, where is my brother? I want to talk to Ace?" I tried to reason with my brother's dark personality.

"Bando ain't here, sis. Bando ain't the one that wants to kill Jayson and you. I do."

I saw that my gun was only a few feet away from me, but so did Ace.

"I wouldn't do that." I felt someone behind me as they pressed a gun to my head.

"Kimberly?" I heard Jayson say.

I knew this bitch didn't just get the drop on me. I didn't even know she knew my brother. I knew she felt some type of way that Jayson divorced her to be with me, but shit that was over twenty-five years ago. I knew this bitch wasn't still pressed. If anything, she should have been pointing a gun at Ace for killing her daughter.

Bitches were weird.

"You working with the nigga that killed our daughter?" Jayson read my mind.

"Trinity was stupid, entitled, and needy. She was a keep-a-nigga baby that didn't pan out. I had her to keep you, and you still left me to go be the R. Kelly of Cuba. So when Ace reached out to me about killing both of y'all, I was with it."

"But the nigga still killed your daughter." I didn't care about her diabolical plan of revenge for some dick she ain't have in a minute. Bitch, how the fuck you just ignore that shit.

"That's irrelevant." Kimberly brushed off my comment.

"She's right. And since we are the ones with the guns, this is about Jayson and you."

"Y'all beef is with me. Not Tia. Let her go. I killed your dad. I'm the one that had Trinity involved for the drops. I'm the one that divorced you. Tia didn't even know I was married."

"You dying too, nigga. The fuck?" Ace commented. "You want to die for her, I'ma respect that. She's gonna die for you too. Shit, she wouldn't even been involved if her ass wouldn't have picked dick over family."

"Nigga, if you gonna kill me, kill me," Jayson taunted.

"Ace, please don't do this, bro," I begged. "You want the money, you can have the fucking money!"

"Is that money going to bring my dad back?" Ace blinked his eyes, revealing that his soul had been long gone.

I didn't even know how to respond. There wasn't enough money in the world to bring Ashton back. And to be honest, Ace didn't know Ashton like that. When Ashton came to America, he forgot about Ace. At this point, my brother was just dead set on killing anybody that he came across. I had not made peace with my maker. I wasn't ready to die.

"Fuck that nigga. Let Tia go. I'm ready to die, but leave my woman out of it."

"You right. Say bye, Tia."

Pow!

I couldn't breathe as I literally saw the bullet lodged into Jayson's skull. I was shaking my head no, like it was going to save Jayson's life. My world slowed down as Jayson's soul left his body.

"Jayson!" I cried. I didn't even get to mourn him as Ace pointed the gun at me. I didn't even have any words to plead for my life. I was selfish. I didn't want to be apart from my kids, but I had no choice in the matter.

Pow, pow!

Blood drenched my face. I quickly rubbed my face and body, and I didn't have one bullet wound. That's when I saw Kimberly dead on the floor.

"I didn't miss." Ace still had his gun pointed at me. "I can't trust no bitch that is willing to work with her daughter's killer. You still my sister, and I'm not about to let some weird bitch shoot you."

I just stood there in shock, looking down at Kimberly's lifeless body. I guess I was next.

"I really wish that you wouldn't have left me in that mental hospital. I didn't just kill mama's boyfriend because he was beating on us. He was touching on me. But how could I publicly say that I was letting another man do nasty shit to me?"

"You was a kid." I cried because Ace had transformed from a killer to the little brother I wasn't able to protect. As I looked back at the signs, they were there. I lived in another city, engrossed with Jayson, and yet the signs of abuse were there. My mom calling saying that she found blood in Ace's underwear. How withdrawn he was when I would come visit. The nightmares. Then he was killing animals, and all the blame went on Ace for being the bad seed. No one questioned that Ace wasn't born a killer, he was made into one. My mom met Paul when Ace was only three years old. I couldn't even imagine what pain my brother endured. "Ace, I'm sorry," I sobbed. "I didn't know. I was so involved with Jayson that I didn't even notice. Baby bro, I'm so sorry."

"You don't get to be sorry, Tia! You left me with that monster. Mama was so scared of him that she acted like she didn't notice. And even then, you treated me like you was embarrassed of me. Isaiah introduced himself to me and didn't even know who I was. I told him my name and everything. But it's all good. I'm not going to be missed. The only one who somewhat gave a fuck was my dad. He was the only one coming to visit me." Ace began to tap his gun against his head. "I love you, Tia. Even though you didn't love me." Ace began to cry.

"I love you too, Ace. I was a child my damn self. But that ain't no excuse for how I was moving. We can get—"

Pow!

Ace's body dropped like a fly to the floor. I rushed over to his body, hoping that he was somewhat alive. But I knew that was a lie as soon as I touched his body. A bitch was heartbroken. I lost the love of my life and my brother all in the same day. I did not wake up this morning thinking Jayson was going to die. And as much as I knew I had to kill Ace, I didn't think I could have killed my baby brother. It didn't even matter now, because I had lost them both.

❦ 26 ❦

SHAWNIE

It's been too long and I'm lost without you
What am I gonna do?
Said I been needin' you, wantin' you
(Said I need you)
Wonderin' if you're the same and who's been with you
Is your heart still mine?
I wanna cry sometimes
I miss you
Now I'm sittin' here
Thinkin' 'bout you
And the days we used to share
It's drivin' me crazy
I don't know what to do
I'm just wonderin' if you still care
I don't wanna let you know
That it's killin' me
I know you got another life you gotta concentrate baby
Come back...to me
Can you...feel me (Callin')
Hear me...callin' (For you)
For you...'Cause it's

It's been too long and I'm lost without you
What am I gonna do?

J aya sang the Aaliyah ballad in the front of the church, and there wasn't a dry eye in sight.

Dejah deserved to go out in style. Tia found a video of Dejah pleading for her life on Ace's phone. Ace killed my baby and my wife. Had the whole world thinking that Dejah killed Jenesis, me included.

I really thought Dejah had snapped. But she remained a good woman all the way to the end. I promise if I met Dejah first and Keisha didn't exist, I could see myself only with her.

"Good morning, everyone," I addressed everyone that was in attendance. "Dejahnae was a woman who loved hard, and you could do nothing but be in awe of her beauty, kindness, and genuine heart. Dejah came into my life when I was going through one of the darkest times in my life. I real talk didn't deserve a woman like her. And it hurts me that both her and my daughter are gone. Rest peacefully, Dejah. Kiss our baby girl for me." I wanted my eulogy to be longer, but I didn't want to lie to these people. I was a horrible husband, and instead of trusting my instinct, I let the narrative of baby killer control how I viewed Dejah.

I pulled out all the stops for Dejah for this funeral to make sure she went out in style. Keisha respected Dejah in death, and we both decided it would be best if she didn't attend the funeral.

The funeral was over and everybody was getting ready to head to the repass, when I found Jaya on the back pew crying.

"Sis, you good?" I knew that Jaya fucked with Dejah, but I knew for a fact that she wasn't crying about my deceased wife.

"You did a good job with this funeral. But you didn't do that for my dad, your uncle."

"You know why, Jay." I sat next to my cousin.

"That still don't make it right."

I knew Jaya was upset about not doing a funeral let alone even burying my uncle Jayson. As nice of an apartment as Ms. Tia had, it still was a trap house. I used to sell drugs, so I knew that having unnecessary attention was redundant, even if it meant you had to get rid of someone you loved's body like trash. My uncle's body wasn't sent to the morgue, a clean-up crew disposed of the body, mafia style. Jaya was upset, but Ms. Tia had to think of business first. Ms. Tia still had to give the money to Ice, and that reup money provided a comfy lifestyle for Jaya and my niece. But I understood Jaya's pain too. A funeral would have been some good closure.

"Okay, we didn't get to have the funeral. But we did have the balloon release. Your dad loved you. And most importantly, y'all was able to reconcile y'all's relationship. That's what matters."

"You right. But now my kids won't have a grandpa now."

"They don't have no grandpa, but they got a uncle that loves them. You ain't alone, Jay. You still got family."

"I know." Jaya wiped her eyes. "I got to go get the kids. Come by the house later."

"Alright, I will."

I spotted Ms. Tomika and tried to give her my condolences. As soon as I got close enough, she hugged me. Then she slapped the shit out of me. "You stood on my porch and promised to look after my only child. You broke her, JaShawn! She was dead inside long before she was killed. You took my only baby and my only grandchild from me. You get to go live your life with your side piece and new baby. But what about me? My whole heart is rotting in the ground."

I hung my head because there was no rebuttal for the truth. I hurt Dejah, and Ms. Tomika was right. Dejah was dead before Ace killed her. "I fucking hate you!" Ms. Tomika began to hit me and scream that it should have been me in the casket and not Dejah. And I let her. Ice and Lil' Way had to restrain her. I felt like shit, and when the repass began, I was nowhere in sight.

❧

THREE MONTHS LATER

My nerves were all over the place. I was so used to shit going wrong that when things went right, I questioned it. I told Keisha that the baby she was carrying was my child regardless if I was the biological dad. But this bitch went and got a prenatal DNA test. And not only was I the father, the baby was a boy.

To say a nigga was ecstatic. But I didn't deserve this blessing with the way I did Dejah. Ms. Tomika was right, I was the reason Dejah was gone. Dejah was killed by association to me. She died with the label of baby killer. And I knew that shit hurt her the most. Her blood was on my hands, and I had no clue why God was blessing me.

And when I say blessings were pouring, they were pouring. Today I was marrying my soul mate. My best friend. The woman who's held my heart since I was eight years old. Keisha. I fought it for so long, but you can't help who you love. The day that Keisha was supposed to marry Bernard, I didn't wake up that morning thinking to ruin their marriage. But I just couldn't allow myself to live without her a moment longer. She was always on my mind, and as much respect as I had for Dejah, I was miserable without Keisha.

You know it's all entertainment (yup)
Some people wanna be famous
I just keep it low, and stack this paper (I count it up)
And roll blunts with my baby, yeah
Ring, ring, ring, ring (hit me up)
Baby, I could be your private thing...

My and Keisha's song began to play. It was not the traditional wedding song, and my mama cussed me behind it. But this was me and Keisha, we were hood. Shit, so was Keyonna. Keisha and I weren't changing who we were.

I stood at the altar of the roof top deck of the Seafair Yacht, waiting with Pastor Norton. The pastor that did me and Keisha's premarital counselling. The first to come down the aisle was my OG, with Israel and Izzy. They were only one year old, so my mom had to help Israel throw the flowers and hold the ring on Izzy's behalf.

Next were Lil' Way and Shanice. I knew Dejah's friend, Shanice, felt some type of way about me. But her love for Lil' Way and her being under the impression that Dejah was killed randomly kept her composure. Not even Lil' Way knew the real truth.

Jaya and Ice were the maids of honor, and my best man came down the aisle right before bae came out.

"May we all stand for the bride..." Pastor Norton advised everyone in attendance.

You took my love and I'm willing
There's no limit to the love I'm giving
The love I'm giving

And then here came out bae. Looking like the queen that she was. Even with her round belly that held my son, she still was looking sexy. I didn't do tears, but a nigga was shedding a few seeing Keisha. Back when we were kids, we used to play house. I was the daddy, Keisha was the mama, and Jaya was the daughter. We even had a wedding. Some kids playing around in the back yard could not compare to this moment right now.

We let my mom pick this old ass song, but I was feeling it as Keisha got closer. Keisha and I fought through so much bullshit to get to this point. But she was worth it. I finally got my heart in human form.

"We are gathered here today to witness and celebrate the marriage of JaShawn and Keisha," Pastor Norton began "This is not the beginning of a new relationship but an acknowledgment of the next chapter in their lives together. JaShawn and Keisha have spent years getting to know each other, and we now bear witness to what their relationship has become. Today, they will affirm this bond formally and publicly. The couple has written their own vows this evening. JaShawn?"

I cleared my throat and recited my vows. "I promise to always strive to meet your needs, not out of obligation, but because it delights me to see you happy.

I promise to be there for you, whenever you need me.

I promise to nurture your goals and ambitions, to support you through misfortune, and to celebrate your triumphs.

I promise to keep our lives exciting, adventurous, and full of passion.

I promise to persevere when times get tough, knowing that any challenges we might face, we will conquer them together.

I promise to treat you with compassion rather than fairness, because we are a team, now and for always.

I promise to show you, every day, that I know exactly how lucky I am to have you in my life.

"I love you, with everything I have. Today I am so proud to call you my wife. Words will never be enough to show the love I have for you. When I'm with you, my heart beats so fast. I feel like it may explode if I let myself feel just how much I love you. The extent of your beauty is overwhelming, both inside and out. I could not possibly live without you. I promise to be there for you and our family, and I will never let you down. I look forward to growing old with you. You are my best friend and my soul-mate. I have loved you since the day I met you, and I will continue to do so until forever.

"You know that there are some things I don't believe in. But today, I want to tell you about some things I do believe in. I believe in sunrises and sunsets. I believe in hikes in the woods and walks on the beach.... I believe in all the beauty, the mystery, and the wonder of life, and I believe that these joys, like all joys, are multiplied when you have someone to share them with. And I'm here because I want you to be that person.

"There's no one else I'd rather spend my life with. I love your shy smile, your sweet laugh, your sense of humor, and your adventurousness. And most of all, I love the way you make me happier than I thought anyone ever could. That's why I'm here, and that's why I'm marrying you today.

"Where there has been cold, you have brought warmth; where there was darkness, you have brought light. Our miracle lies in the path we have chosen together. I enter this marriage with you, knowing that the true magic of love is not to avoid changes, but to follow the path together, hand in hand. Let us commit to the miracle of making each day work, together.

"Whatever lies ahead, good or bad, we will face together. Distance may test us for a time, and time may try us. But if we look to each other first, we will always see a friend. For better or worse, richer or poorer, in sickness and health, in joy and in sorrow, to love and to cherish, to be faithful to you alone.

"I promise to love you without reservation, comfort you in times of distress, encourage you to achieve all of your goals, laugh with you and cry with you, grow with you in mind and spirit, always be open and honest with you, and cherish you for as long as we both shall live. You are my best friend, and my soulmate, I have loved you since the day I met you, and I will continue to do so until forever."

"Keisha?" Pastor Norton turned his attention to Keisha.

"You know that there are some things I don't believe in. But today, I want to tell you about some things I do believe in. I believe in sunrises and sunsets. I believe in hikes in the woods and walks on the beach. I believe in all the beauty, the mystery and the wonder of life, and I believe that these joys, like all joys, are multiplied when you have someone to share them with. And I'm here because I want you to be that person. There's no one else I'd rather spend my life with. I love your shy smile, your sweet laugh, your sense of humor, and your adventurousness. And most of all, I love the way you make me happier than I thought anyone ever could. That's why I'm here, and that's why I'm marrying you today.

"So this is love, so this is what makes life divine. I'm all aglow and now I know the key to all heaven is mine. My heart has wings and I can fly, I'll touch the star in every sky. So this is the miracle that I've been dreaming of. So this is love.

I promise to encourage your compassion,
Because that is what makes you unique and wonderful.
I promise to nurture your dreams,
Because through them your soul shines.
I promise to help shoulder our challenges,
For there is nothing we cannot face if we stand together.
I promise to be your partner in all things,
Not possessing you, but working with you as a part of the whole.

Lastly, I promise to you perfect love and perfect trust,
For one lifetime with you could never be enough.
This is my sacred vow to you, my equal in all things.
I promise to encourage your individuality,
Because that is what makes you unique and wonderful.
I promise to nurture your dreams,
Because through them your soul shines.
I promise to help shoulder our challenges,
Because through them we'll emerge stronger.
I promise to be your partner in all things,
Not possessing you, but working with you as a part of the whole.

I promise to share with you the joys of life,
Because with you they will be that much sweeter.

I wanna make you smile whenever you're sad, carry you around when your arthritis is bad, all I wanna do is grow old with you. I'll get your medicine when your tummy aches, build you a fire if the furnace breaks, oh it could be so nice, growing old with you. I'll miss you, kiss you, give you my coat when you are cold. Need you, feed you, even let you hold the remote control. So let me do the dishes in our kitchen sink, put you to bed when you've had too much to drink, oh I could be the woman who grows old with you, I wanna grow old with you.

Lastly, I promise to you perfect love and perfect trust,
For one lifetime with you could never be enough.
This is my sacred vow to you, my equal in all things."

"What God has joined together, let no man put asunder. Having pledged their fidelity to one another, to love, honor, and cherish one another in the presence of this gathering and by the authority vested in me by the constitution and the laws of this state, it is my honor to now pronounce you husband and wife. You may kiss the bride."

Everybody yelled out congratulations instead of Happy New Year, as fireworks set off in the backdrop, letting the world know that we were now Mr. and Mrs. Mitchell.

🦋 27 🦋

ICE

"Hello?" I answered my phone with skepticism. I didn't like strange numbers.

"Is this Isaiah Green?" I didn't like strangers calling me by my whole government.

"Who the fuck is this?" I got angry.

"My name is Gina. I'm calling about my client, Hennessy."

"I don't know no damn Hennessy," I said with short patience.

"I know you don't know, sir, but she is willing to pay for you."

"Pay for what?"

"For sexual services and—"

I wasn't with the bullshit, and I was highly offended that some hoe was offering me pussy through the phone. I wasn't the most upstanding nigga, but creeping on Jaya wasn't me. "Look here, bitch, you and Cîroc—"

"Hennessy."

"Whatever the fuck her name is. You tell that bitch she can keep that thirsty pussy. I'm very appalled that you or this bitch thought that I was slanging dick. You hoes—"

The woman started laughing. "Baby, it's me!"

"Jaya?"

"Yes!"

"Man, who the fuck is this?"

"Baby, it's me!"

"Nah man, quit playing."

The woman on the other line changed her voice.

"Jay?"

"Yes! I was trying to roll play."

"Ah shit, sorry babe. I done called you a bitch."

"It's all good. It just let me know you for me only. So what's up, Mr. Green, can my client see you tonight? Jaya went back into roll play mode and I was all with it.

"How much she trying to pay? Because this dick ain't cheap." Both Jaya and I laughed.

"I've heard. Can you meet her at..."Jaya ranted off our address.

"Yup, what time?"

"Seven."

I was excited for a nice dinner at home with Jaya and the kids, maybe get my dick sucked. But as soon as I pulled up at the house at the allocated time Jaya gave me, there was a red carpet that led from our front door to an Uber car. I chuckled because Jaya was determined to give it a little hood twist. I loved it.

"Mr. Green?" she called as she walked out of the house.

"Yes, Gina?"

"No. Gina is my assistant. I'm Hennessey."

"Damn, she didn't say you was going to be this fine. I thought only ugly bitches bought dick." Jaya playfully pushed me.

"Actually, I'm a busy businesswoman. I don't have time for relationships. I just want dick. No strings attached."

"Damn, ok." I admired Jaya, she was looking good as fuck. Her blue dress was hugging every curve and her eyes settled into a greenish gray.

"Are you ready?" Jaya put her hand out, and I thought we were going to a restaurant, but the Uber driver pulled up to the airport. I still wasn't understanding what was going on, until Jaya led me to the United Airlines check-in.

"Where we going?"

"Mr. Green, don't worry, you're in good hands, just enjoy yourself. Trust me, it's well worth it." My baby wanted to show out and I was going to let her. I could not keep my hands off of Jaya once we got on the plane. We were about to have first class lit as fuck as I found my hand under Jaya's dress.

"You better stop," moaned Jaya as she slid back and forth on my finger.

"Come to the bathroom," I suggested as I removed my hand.

"Okay."

I went in first then Jaya came in with me. There was not a lot of room, so I lifted Jaya up around my waist, leaning her back against the wall of the bathroom. Jaya acted like she just got out of a women's convent the way she was moaning and squirting on my dick.

Jaya was moaning so loud that I had to cover up her mouth with my hand. But I didn't slow down my stroke game as I dug into Jaya with vicious power. I was trying to be the man, but the way that Jaya was cumming back to back, I was about to nut too.

Bam Bam

"I need to use the restroom!" someone shouted from the other side of the door.

But Jaya and I were in another world as she whispered in my ear, "Don't stop."

Fuck who was on the other side of the door, as my and Jaya bodies liquidated into sexual bliss. "Marry me?" I let Jaya's body go, standing her up gently.

She giggled. "Baby, we are already engaged." Jaya dangled her hand in my face with the diamond ring on her finger.

"No, when we get to wherever we going. Marry me, Jaya."

"But what about our family?"

I didn't know what it was, but I realized I couldn't go another day without making Jaya Mrs. Green. We been through the bullshit, but our love stayed true. She was the first woman I didn't want to cheat on. I knew what I had at home. Jaya was a little bit rough around the edges. She was good as it came, but she was loyal, and she made me feel like I was a king. Every day I came home, the house was decent and she was starting on dinner. But we had two small kids and one on the way, so it was a fight to keep the house perfect. She was always happy to see me, and whatever I was battling in the streets, she was my peace. It had nothing to do with her looks or the sex, it was her, period.

"We can do something when we come back. Like a reception."

"Ok, let's do—"

"I have to use the bathroom!" the voice said again from the other side of the door.

"Sorry about that," I said after we got ourselves cleaned up and opened the door.

"Y'all are just nasty. This ain't no brothel. There are kids on here," the black woman lectured us, as we tried not to laugh.

"Yes, ma'am," Jaya and I both said as we bypassed her to get back to our seats.

"This ain't no brothel!" I joked as we plopped down in our seats, and we both chuckled.

"We really about to do this, huh?"

"Yes, I mean, you getting scared?"

"No, I'm actually happy." Jaya smiled as she leaned into me and rested her head on my chest.

I was excited about our destination as we made it to Hawaii. I had my passport in the safe but Jaya wasn't able to get it, so she settled for Hawaii. But I was happy with her choice regardless of what she picked.

We weren't on the Big Island for more than two hours before we were standing only feet away from the Pacific Ocean as I was ready to declare both my love and fidelity to Jaya. Money talked and bullshit walked as I paid for this quick wedding. The hotel made it happen as I watched Jaya walk barefoot down the aisle of flowers.

> *Baby while we're young*
> *I think we should do something crazy*
> *Like say "Fuck everyone"*
> *And just run away from the daily routine*
> *Yeah you know what I mean*
> *I'm tellin' everybody you're mine and I like it*
> *And I really hope you don't mind, I can't fight it*
> *No, you know I cannot hide it 'cause I am so excited*
> *That I finally decided on you*
> *'Cause it's been another perfect day with ya*
> *Wanna lay with ya*
> *Spend the night with ya*
> *Then spend my life with ya, alright*
> *Alright, alright*
> *Yeah you heard me right*
> *I'll go everywhere you go (I'll go everywhere you go)*
> *You know I'll go, I'll go*
> *Everywhere you go (I'll go everywhere you go)*
> *You know I'll go, I'll go*
> *Everywhere you go (I'll go everywhere you go*
> *You know I'll go, I'll go)*
> *Everywhere you go (I'll go everywhere you go)*
> *You know I'll go, I'll go*

Jhene Aiko must have known how I was feeling as I watched Jaya walk toward me. Jaya looked like heaven as she wore a soft white sundress, her hair was in some fancy bun shit, and her creamy skin was sun-kissed by the Hawaiian sun. I didn't give a fuck what she wore, I was smashing my wife after the ceremony.

This was it. I was marrying the woman of my dreams. I fell in love with her the moment she cussed me out when she first got out of jail.

"Do you want to start?" the minister stated as he looked at me.

SOMEONE TO CALL BAE 3

I cleared my throat and began. "Love has never felt so good. I can't imagine my life without you or the kids. I was grown before, but you helped me to be the man I have become. Man, this shit got me all in my feelings, bruh. What can I say? A nigga ain't never been in love like I love you. I knew that day you came to the door cussing me out that you were the one. But it wasn't just you. I fell in love with our kids. Yo, you made a nigga work hard, but it was worth it. I promise, Jaya, to be that nigga to hold it down, to hold your hand every night, and to never let us lose our spark."

I winked to let Jaya know that I would never give her that weak dick. "No matter what I do in these streets, this dick will always be yours and yours only. I vow to not entertain any thots, hoes, sluts, or whatever. No bitch from the time we got together can say I tried to get with them. You got my muthafuckin' heart, girl! And my bread, shit. I ain't never been no settle down type nigga. But I'm happy to do that shit for you. I muthafuckin' got you, babe. I mean that shit. To the death of me. You and my kids are all I care about. I'll lie, ride, die about y'all. Real talk. I love you like a fat boy loves cake. Just know you getting muthafuckin' pregnant tonight!" Even though Jaya was already pregnant, I was going fuck her like I was trying to get her pregnant.

The minister looked at me all crazy, but I gave no fucks. I had a few cocktails on the plane, but that's how I felt from my heart. This shit was real. I was a hood nigga in love with my bae. Muthafucka knew not to say shit because my money was right, and if he did, I would have beat his ass. I focused on Jaya, and tears were coming from her eyes. As long as she knew how I felt, I didn't give a fuck about the next nigga.

"Awww, babe!" Jaya gushed.

"Jaya, please state your vows," the minister instructed Jaya.

"Isaiah Green, I love you with all my heart. You like the hood Prince Charming. I was going through so much when we made it official. Homeless, sleeping on Shawnie's air mattress, and pregnant. I been really hurt by my ex-husband. No, fuck that, you my only husband. Fuck that nigga. But you know what I mean. But then you came along and changed my whole world. I ain't never been no bum bitch, but I wasn't living my full potential. You showed me, babe, this new life. I thank you for seeing me at my lowest and not giving up on me. I know I was dumb as fuck. But I'm for you and only you. I promise to try to keep the house clean, most days, suck yo' dick, be a lady in the streets and a porn star in the sheets. To be your ride or die. I know this shit with our family has been some bullshit. But, babe, I love you and I choose you. Fuck everybody else. It's me, you, and these kids. Oh, and you got me fucked up. You ain't getting me pregnant. Because, nigga, I'm already pregnant. Love you!"

"Wow, okay." The minister looked embarrassed.

Fuck him.

"I now pronounce you husband and wife. You may now kiss your bride!" the minister announced as I brought Jaya close to me and kissed her. The hotel staff blew bubbles as we walked back down the aisle to go to our room. All I knew was that Jaya was now mine.

❧ 28 ❧

JAYA

FINAL CHAPTER

FOUR MONTHS LATER

"I was meaning to ask you. What happened to Mr. Otis?"

"He tried to sue me for the cost of the wedding and my engagement ring."

"What?" I gasped.

"That is until Shawnie paid him a visit. That nigga went ghost after that."

Keisha's newborn baby began to stir from his sleep, and I picked him up. "Him getting so big!" I cooed at my nephew, Julian.

"I swear this is my one and only child. 'Cause, girl, I don't even remember the last time I slept," Keisha replied as I got comfortable in Keisha's bed. "Then my dumb ass is breastfeeding, so no weed or Crown."

"At least you had the baby. My ass still got a few weeks to go."

"So you not going to find out what you're having?" Keisha asked for the umpteenth time.

"You know you ask me this shit almost every fucking day? Me and Isaiah want it to be a surprise."

"That's stupid."

"You know how my last gender reveal went. I don't want no more secrets popping up."

I was ready for a nap since Ms. Tia had the twins. Any trace of Izzy's maternal side was gone. There was no point to telling Izzy that his mama was my sister. His daddy was my ex-husband. And that his adoptive daddy's uncle killed his grandma. Just like it wasn't point to tell Israel about Trap Star. Isaiah and I decided that since our kids were only two weeks apart, we picked one day for their birthday. It made shit easier.

"I guess. You hungry? Shawnie bringing home dinner."

"Hell yeah!"

"Bitch, I know you just didn't pee in my bed?"

I wasn't following until I felt the warm liquid myself. This was the worst time for my water to break. Isaiah was damn near across the country. He loved him some Izzy and Israel, but this child would be his firstborn, and I wanted my husband here to witness our baby entering the world.

As soon as I went into my contacts to call Isaiah, a contraction ripped through my body, causing me to double over.

"Shawnie!" Keisha yelled, her voice filling with urgency.

"You... The fuck is all that?" Shawnie got horrified. I didn't want my cousin to see me like this, but these contractions were hurting so bad that I would not care about delivering this baby right here in their bed.

"She's in labor. Help me get her into your car." Keisha held Julian in one arm while trying to maneuver me to stand.

"You got me fucked up, Zo. She is not getting in my car, peeing out baby juice."

"Well, how else? Because Mama got my car," Keisha relayed about Auntie Key using her car.

"We can't get her into an Uber or an ambulance?"

"You better do something before I have this baby in y'all's bed! Ahhh," I screamed as another contraction hit. I didn't remember this kind of pain with Israel.

"Nigga, go get the fucking keys!" Keisha snapped on Shawnie.

"I got you, sis." Keisha helped me off the bed. I was panting like when I made this muthafucka. But nothing was pleasurable about active labor.

I almost forgot to call my husband. "The baby is coming," I managed to say.

"Damn, for real? What hospital you at? I'm on my way."

"I'm on my way to Jackson Memorial—"

Keisha snatched the phone from me. "I don't know how you going to get here, but this baby is coming."

"Fuck!" Isaiah said through the speaker. "I'm coming, babe."

Shawnie and Keisha argued the whole time to the hospital about me ruining his back seat. Soon as I had this baby, me and Shawnie were going to fight. Nigga, fuck your seats. It seemed like forever to get to the hospital as my baby tried to rip through me.

As soon as I got into the hospital, I was rushed up to labor and delivery. I was trying so hard for this baby not to come until Isaiah came. But the way this pain was hitting, I needed this demon child out of me ASAP. The pain wasn't matching the slowness of being dilated. When I got here, I was only at a four. There's no way I was in this much pain and only dilated to four. That was five hours ago, and the epidural they gave me was not helping shit.

"Jaya, the baby is crowning. It's time to push," the nurse addressed me.

"I can't!" I cried.

"Sis, you got this." Keisha grabbed my hand since Shawnie's scary ass insisted on waiting in the waiting room with Julian.

"I wanted to wait for Isaiah," I whined, but the urge to push trumped that.

"On this next contraction, Jaya, I want you to push."

A contraction hit me and I bore down to push. "Ahhh!" I yelled.

"This baby is going to have a lot of hair." The nurse patted my leg.

"I can't keep going. I'm tired."

"We are almost there. Here comes another contraction. Come on, Jaya, push."

"You got this." I looked up to see Isaiah, Auntie Key, and Ms. Tia.

I smiled weakly as I pushed.

"Keep pushing."

"Whaaaa!" I heard my baby cry, and it was the sweetest sound I'd ever heard.

"It's a boy!"

The nurses placed my little prince on my chest as they wiped him down, and Isaiah cut the cord.

I sat cradled in Isaiah's arms as he kissed my forehead and admired our son in my arms. He was cute, as he was the spitting image of Isaiah with his gray eyes and brownish black hair. I was so in love.

"What y'all going to name him?" Keisha asked.

"Jayson." Isaiah, Ms. Tia, Auntie Key, and myself said at the same time.

☿

"You alright?" I watched Ms. Tia stare out my living room window. Her eyes were glossy and not responsive.

"Yeah. No." Ms. Tia finally acknowledged me. "I really loved your daddy. I wasn't ready to die. He wasn't either. I miss him every day."

"I know you do. So do I."

"I even miss my brother," Ms. Tia admitted.

I didn't respond. I knew what it meant to lose someone that you loved but didn't always do what was right, aka my dad. I was just glad that we were able to reconcile our relationship before he died. I felt bad for Ms. Tia that she didn't get the same chance. I actually felt sorry for Ace because he was so mentally disturbed. If only he got the help that he needed, he would have had a better outcome.

"Your dad would have wanted you to have this." Ms. Tia pulled an envelope out of her purse. "Back when we were married, we bought some property. I kept it after the divorce. But I think it's only right that you have it."

I looked down at the piece of paper that held some commercial space. It was a blessing because I had just passed my real estate exam and I wanted to open my own business, but I was scared to take the leap. But now this was a sign that I was on the right path.

"Thank you!" I hugged Ms. Tia. "Ms. Tia, you just don't know—"

"Girl, if you don't stop calling me Ms. Tia."

"What do you want me to call you?"

"Ma. Tia. T. But Ms. Tia is so formal, you family."

"Thank you, Ma." I let the words slip out.

"Better. And then there's this." Tia pulled out some pictures. "These were in your dad's safe."

It was like looking at a mirror. I really looked like my mother. I had never seen a picture of her, but she had my whole face. These pictures were more valuable than the property. I continued to stare at the pictures when Tia stood up to leave.

"I have to get Isis and Indica. You coming to their graduation?"

"I will be there."

"I know you got your auntie, but if you need me, I'm here too." Tia rubbed my back.

I looked up briefly at Tia before bringing my attention back to the pictures. I thought I couldn't miss a person I didn't remember, but seeing my mom, I realized that there was a part of me that would always belong to her.

I was laying on the couch with little Jayson on my chest, watching Isaiah play with Izzy and Israel. I didn't know what it was, but I loved how my babies laughed. I loved how Isaiah would come home from a long day of work and still make time for me and the kids.

I was so happy that my baby officially was legit. I didn't know if Isaiah could handle being an employee. His ass wouldn't last a week, clocking in for another muthafucka. I think Isaiah knew that shit too. So my baby created himself his own job. He became the owner of his trucking company. He didn't have a huge fleet, but fifteen trucks and drivers brought in good money. Even Isaiah's mama was out. She had saved over the last twenty years and invested. Her ass didn't have to work a day in her life.

"Come on, y'all." I tried to sit up. "It's bedtime."

"I got it." Isaiah picked up the baby and ushered Israel and Izzy upstairs.

I was at work all day selling houses, and then came home to three kids under two. A bitch was tired every day, and so I cherished when Isaiah helped out. I got up from the couch and went into our room to take a shower. I tried to wait for Isaiah, but as soon as I got under the covers, I was out.

I woke the next morning snuggled next to Isaiah.

"Good morning." I kissed Isaiah's lips.

"Good morning. Get dressed."

"I will. I just got to get the kids ready to go to daycare."

"They ain't here."

I looked at my phone and it was 9 am. "What do you mean they ain't here?"

"My mom came and got them."

That made my morning easier as I prepared to get ready for the day, but Isaiah stopped me. "Pack light, we out this bitch."

"Uh, what about our kids?" I looked at Isaiah crazy.

"They good. The last time we had some time to ourselves, you was pregnant."

"How long we going to be gone?"

"Just five days."

TWO HOURS LATER

"Babe, this shit is gorgeous!" I looked at the skyline from the deck of the yacht we were on. Isaiah had me spoiled as he treated me to a yacht trip to the Bahamas.

"It was my idea." I turned to see Keisha and Shawnie getting on the boat.

"Ignore him." Keisha rolled her eyes. "You looking cute, bitch."

"You know how I do. You looking cute too."

"Girl, tell me why this nigga almost had us miss the boat." Keisha side eyed Shawnie.

"Nah, that was your fault." Shawnie pulled Keisha into him. "Round four?"

"Come on, babe." I pulled Isaiah toward the belly of the ship. I didn't want to see my cousin being nasty. "Where's our room at?"

"To the right." Isaiah steered me from behind. "It's near theirs, but the rooms are soundproof."

That was music to my ears. You would have thought that I'd never seen any nice shit the way I was so impressed by some damn flowers in a vase.

"I can't believe you did all this." I looked around as Isaiah wrapped his arms around me from behind, kissing my neck.

"You deserve it."

I didn't respond as I turned around to kiss my husband. I was transformed into the thirteen-year-old girl having a crush on her cousin's best friend. My and Isaiah's love had real life been through the fire. And there was no man I would want to get it out of the mud with other than Isaiah.

Three years ago, I was walking into my house with my supposed best friend and finding out she was fucking my husband. It didn't seem like it at the time, but it was best thing that ever happened to me. I forgot my roots, I forgot about the people that loved me. Coming back to Miami broke, homeless, and pregnant, humbled my ass. It made me appreciate life more, instead of being the spoiled, naïve brat I used to be.

I'd endured so much heartache in these last three years that I didn't think it would ever get better. I knew that I had fucked up too many times and almost lost Isaiah. I was counting my blessings every day, and I lived my life not taking Isaiah or my kids for granted. I would always miss my dad. I wished he was still here. I had family that loved me. And more importantly, I had someone to call bae.

The End

CPSIA information can be obtained
at www.ICGtesting.com
Printed in the USA
LVHW030937211121
704027LV00003B/472